Praises

MW01484966

"*Great book from a real storyteller. Anyone who knows and loves America's heartland will nod and smile at the fine details woven delicately through the tapestry of this story's Missouri setting. Anyone who loves characters who are as real as the people you have actually met will appreciate the way Hooper's characters come to life and stay alive in your memory.*"
--Robin Blakely, author of SIX HATS and PR THERAPY

My criteria for a five start review is this: do I keep turning pages when I should be doing something else? The Possessor met that criteria. David Hooper has penned a coming of age tale that gently leads the reader through the trials of Mac, a young boy who is sent to live in the country with his aunt after his father has a stroke. Placed in what I assume is the 50s, Hooper slid me into the story gently with a writing style that is deceptively simple. It doesn't take long, though, to realize that the author has painted a picture of place , time, and character so expertly that the work only seems effortless. Beyond the incredible attention to detail, is the way the plot builds and surprises in the end. This coming of age experience is one I never saw coming and that twist was the best of all. The conclusion was one I accepted all the while wondering how the characters were going to live with themselves. What could be better than a book that leaves you worrying about people who only exist on the page? The cherry on top is how Mr. Hooper writes women. All of his characters are three dimensional and unique, but Aunt Holly is one who will live in my memory for a good long time. I cannot recommend The Possessor highly enough.
--Rebecca Forster, *USA Today's Bestselling Author*

THE POSSESSOR

DAVID M. HOOPER

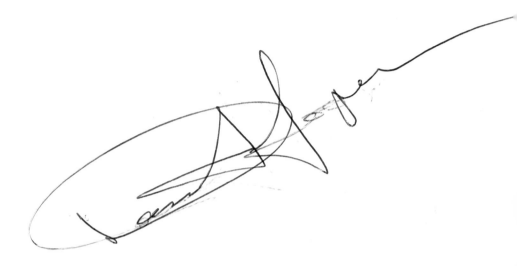

First published by David M. Hooper in 2012.

This is a work of fiction. All characters and events portrayed in this book are fictional, and any resemblance to real people or incidents is purely coincidental.

Cover design and layout by Design Cat Studio. www.designcatstudio.com

The Possessor
David M. Hooper
Copyright David M. Hooper 2011
ISBN-13: 978-1470002169
ISBN-10: 1470002167

1

The rooms are filled with boxes, each one holding memories that won't let go of me. I walk through the old house one last time trying to ignore the lives packed away in cardboard boxes, but I can't help reminiscing. The creaking floor has a welcoming sound that brings a smile to my face. The familiar mustiness of time that goes with all old houses in the country tickles my nose, a smell that unleashes memories of the loved ones who once walked these rooms. The coal oil stove was replaced with a propane wall furnace years ago but it left behind its pungent odor. The pictures have been stripped from the walls and the only furniture left is an old rocking chair that once sat on the porch. I'd spent many hours in that chair reading a book, talking to John, Aunt Holly, and Dory. I have good memories of my loved ones. Memories of an innocent time in my life that are part of the mettle that made me who I am today. This was a time when you didn't grow up so fast that you left your childhood behind before it was over.

As I enter the kitchen with its empty shelves, I find only an old broken kitchen chair to tell me that this room once was filled with laughter. I go to the sink and look out the kitchen window. There is the pond with the old willow tree at one end. That old tree was planted before I was born and will edge that pond after I'm gone. A dock used to be on the south side and stuck out in the water about ten feet. I told Dory I'd replace it when it started to fall apart. She said no. She was glad it was gone because it brought back memories best forgotten. I think she was right about the dock. Neither one us ever walked on that dock again after what happened. Now I've returned for one last pilgrimage before this house slips from my life. I go back to the living room and sit in the old rocking chair to wait for the sound of my children's car. I gently rock back and forth, close my eyes, and let my mind slip back in time to when I was young and I met Dory.

Like many fourteen-year-old boys, it began with baseball dreams filling my head with visions of becoming the next Mickey Mantle or Ted Williams. I got a new baseball glove for Christmas. My best friend, Bob Miller, and I had been throwing the ball and practicing our batting in a small park on Hagerwood Road since late April. In late May, we tried out for the team sponsored by Town Topic hamburgers. The manager chose me to play center field. Bob would pitch and play left field. We knew that this year we would win the league championship that had barely escaped us last year.

We had spent endless hours planning a summer filled with baseball, sleepovers, splashing the girls at the swimming pool at Swope Park or sneaking into the local amusement park. They were innocent times, good times. What followed that summer changed my life forever. The years have passed and all the major participants of that summer are now gone except me. I am the only one left to tell the truth of what really happened that summer.

My family lived in a small, two-bedroom bungalow in a working class neighborhood in south Kansas City. My dad delivered milk and my mother sold real estate part-time. I had one older brother who worked in St. Louis for an insurance company. It all started on a lazy Sunday morning before Sunday school and church. Friday had been my last day of school. My mother talked about how she couldn't believe I'd be a sophomore in high school next year. All I could talk about was my summer vacation.

We'd just finished breakfast. My mother had gone in the bathroom to take a bath before church. I'd gone outside to get the Sunday paper for my dad. It was a cool morning for June. The weatherman predicted rain later in the day and then an unusually hot and humid week. A stiff wind blew in from the Northwest and the sun played hide and seek with dark cotton ball clouds that tumbled across the sky. Sunday morning was usually quiet on Montgall Street except for the occasional car on its way to church. The majority of our neighbors worked as laborers or owned small businesses.

I glanced up the street and saw Mr. Miller, my best friend's father, saunter out their front door in his boxer underwear to get the morning newspaper. He picked up the newspaper, untied the string, and headed back toward his house reading the front page. I found our newspaper on the driveway lying opened. The sections were scattered and the edges fluttered in the light breeze as if they were going to take flight. A well-placed foot kept them in place until I could retrieve them and put them in order. I scampered back into the house and plopped the paper on the kitchen table. My dad had just poured another cup of coffee. He looked up and a slight smile crept to his lips when I walked into the kitchen. Because he woke up six days a week at four-thirty every morning to deliver milk, Sunday was the only day my dad had the time to sit and read the paper. He bent over the table in his wife-beater undershirt, his starched white shirt draped carefully over the back of the chair next to him. He greedily picked through the sections until he found the sports section, delicately picking it out as if he'd found the Dead Sea Scrolls. I sat across the table and waited patiently while he found the comics and tossed them on the table for me to read. This had become a Sunday morning ritual since he'd finished expanding the kitchen. We used to eat in the dining room because the kitchen was so small.

My father was of average height and weight. He had high cheekbones, dark black hair, and the sun had darkened his skin like brown shoe leather. A quiet man with no vices, I don't think I really knew my father in 1954, although we were both working on improving that situation. It was only later that he would become my best friend.

I sat down at the kitchen table and finished the leftover toast on my plate while reading the comics. I ate slowly, relishing every bite. The comics I'd reread two or three times. I had a habit of taking longer to eat my breakfast on Sunday than any other day. I hated Sunday school. My father would finally peer around the corner of the paper to check on my progress. He realized that I would need a nudge to take my shower and get ready for church.

"Hadn't you better go in and finish getting ready for church?" he'd ask.

"I guess," I'd mumble.

I remember being excited that particular morning as I picked up my plate and carried it over to the sink. Bob Miller told me he had the latest issue of Sports News. This issue had an article about the Philadelphia Athletics baseball team moving to Kansas City for the 1955 season. We'd sit together in the balcony during church services. Usually we played mundane games like connect the dots or tic-tac-toe. I hurriedly scraped the remains on my plate into a coffee can sitting in the sink, sat it down on the counter, and headed toward the bathroom.

With only two bedrooms, I'd shared a bed with my brother until he left for his new job in St. Louis. Our living room dining room combination was smaller than most living rooms. Our bathroom sat between our two bedrooms. That morning the bathroom door stood ajar. I peeked in to see my mother at the bathroom sink. She'd just finished brushing her teeth.

"I'll be out in a minute," she said looking at me in the mirror.

The warm, moist heat left over from her bath felt good. Racing into my bedroom, I tore off my clothes, threw them on the floor like any good fourteen-year-old, and hurried to the bathroom in my underwear. Five minutes later, I tumbled out of the bathroom with wet hair, a loose towel wrapped around my waist, and a trail of wet footprints on the hardwood floor. My mother had come out of her bedroom. She stopped and pointed at the floor with a disgusted look on her face.

"Mac, you've got water all over this floor. I want you to go in the kitchen and get the mop and clean up this mess."

"Okay, mom. Wait a second. Let me get my clothes on."

My mother was the opposite of my father. With blue eyes, an outgoing personality, and natural blonde hair, she was a looker. When we'd take the bus downtown, all the men in the bus would stare at her. On Sunday she always wore bright red lipstick. She'd stand in front of the mirror in her bedroom and contort her mouth, carefully following the curve of her lips. Then she'd take the Avon perfume sitting on her dresser and spritz her neck a couple of time and then her wrists. Although I didn't believe it at the time, my mother was the glue that kept our family together. She worked part-time selling real estate when most women stayed in the home. She was good with figures and many of the other real estate agents would come by the house to ask my mother for help.

I dropped the wet towel on the floor and raced to my dresser for underwear. I'd just pulled the tee shirt over my head when I heard mother scream.

. I found my mother in the kitchen on her knees beside my dad. Her hands cupped his shoulders and she was shaking him. My dad's head bobbed up and down like an apple in water. His mouth hung open as if he were drunk. One look at mom's panic-stricken face and I knew it was serious. While I stood in the doorway, quiet and helpless, my mom searched frantically for words.

"You want me to call for an ambulance?" I asked.

"Yes. Tell them to hurry," she said in a hushed voice, tears streaming down her face. Her Sunday morning mascara made black tracks through the red rouge on her cheeks.

2

A shrill whistle split the air of the black night. The railcar jerked back and forth as the train slowed. The metal wheels screeched against the steel tracks like fingernails across a blackboard. I made out a grain silo on one side of the track hidden behind a string of flatcars piled high with hay bales. I pushed my face against the window and saw the lights from the train station and an empty platform. No one was there to meet me. The conductor, a large man with his uniform jacket unbuttoned and his cap tilted back on his head, walked with a stoop down the aisle. His large, black hands alternately touched the backs of the seats. He stopped beside me, leaned forward and spoke in his most official voice.

"This is Bolivar, Missouri young man."

I nodded and slid out of my seat to get my bag from the overhead. He already had it in his hand, waiting for me. I glanced at the few other passengers in the car. The woman behind me looked up, smiled, and then continued reading her magazine. Three men across the aisle were gazing out their windows into the darkness.

I felt so alone.

My father lay in a hospital in Kansas City. My mother and I had followed in the car to the emergency room. It wasn't busy on Sunday morning. The hospital was hot. Oscillating fans lined the halls and circulated a continuous stream of hot air. Curtains stood motionless in front of opened and screened windows. A lazy ceiling fan hung in the middle of the waiting room. I wondered how it could be so nice outside and so hot inside. Mother and I sat huddled together, hands clasped, and waited anxiously for word of my father. My mother had answered a few questions and a short, solemn nurse had then escorted us to the waiting room. Time dragged on forever. My mother would glance at the wristwatch my father had bought her for her birthday and then turn to me and gently caress my hair.

"He's going to be all right," she whispered, crystal tears brimming her eyelids.

"I know," I mumbled.

My mother would look away and dab at her eyes with a handkerchief.

People joined us in the waiting room only to have some doctor or nurse walk into the room, talk to the family, and then they'd all leave.

"Why don't they tell us something," I moaned, wiggling on the hard wooden chair.

"I don't know, honey. Maybe they don't know yet. They'll come and tell us in due time. We have to be patient and pray for your father."

"I've been praying," I answered. "God hasn't said anything yet."

My mother had given me a stern look.

"Don't be flippant, Mac. God doesn't work on our time schedule."

It was ages before a doctor came into the waiting room. He wore green scrubs and a white cap on his head. Long creases, like two large parenthesis, outlined the grim expression on his mouth. He stopped to glance at me before he spoke.

"Mrs. Porter?"

My mother stood up, her hands clasped tightly together.

"Yes?"

"Your husband is stabilized. He is breathing on his own and his heart seems normal."

"Oh thank, God!"

"We need to run a few more tests before we are certain about what's wrong."

"Will I be able to see my husband?" she asked.

"After a while. We're moving him to ICU right now but I don't think he'll be there for long."

She'd buried her face in her hands and began to cry when the doctor left. I'd never seen my mother cry like this. Her shoulders shook and the tears ran down her cheeks like rain. I placed my hand on her back to comfort her. She reached out and gave me a hug.

"Isn't that wonderful, Mac? Your dad is going to be all right."

Later, a nurse summoned my mother to speak with the doctor.

"Mac, you stay right here. I'll be back."

A Life magazine sat on a table to my left and I impatiently flipped through the pictures while I waited. The last couple drifted out of the waiting room and I was alone. I tossed the magazine aside and squirmed in my chair. I didn't see why I couldn't see my dad. Did they think I carried some disease or something? My mother finally returned and asked me to give her a Time magazine. We said little to each other until my grandfather entered the waiting room and sat down beside her.

My grandfather was a tall man for his time. Born at the turn of the twentieth century, he'd grown to be six foot four inches tall, which was a monster back then. He was my mom's dad; he and my grandmother had moved to Kansas City to be near my folks. A gray, bushy mustache adorned his upper lip, a source of pride since before he'd married my grandmother. Everyone tried to get him to shave it off but he wouldn't have it. "This is me," he'd say. My mom called him the gentle giant.

"His bag is in the car," he told my mom quietly. "His grandma packed it. If he needs anything else he can buy it in Bolivar. I put some money in his suitcase."

A look of relief came over my mother. She wiped her eyes and faced me.

Placing both hands on my shoulders, she said, "Mac, I want you to go with your grandfather. He is going to take you to the train station and put you on the train for Bolivar. I want you to stay with my brother, John."

"I don't want to go," I'd pleaded. "Let me stay with you and grandpa."

"Your grandmother is not feeling well, Mac, and I am going to work to help pay the bills. Between work, keeping house, and helping your dad, I just can't handle it," she replied gently.

"I won't be any problem, mom. I promise!"

My pleas were ignored. I was taken out of the hospital and placed on the train despite my tears. I felt betrayed by my family, especially my mother. Surely there was something that could have been done so I didn't have to leave my friends, my summer, and my dad.

"Bolivar, Missouri," the conductor yelled as he started down the aisle with my bag, "next stop, Springfield, Missouri."

I grabbed my glove from the seat and my baseball rolled across the seat onto the floor. At that moment I never imagined I wouldn't pick that glove up again for the rest of the summer. The man across the aisle chuckled, scooped up the ball and handed it to me. I hurried after the conductor. He opened the door to the vestibule and the rocking and squealing of the rail car increased. It was cooler out there and I welcomed the air.

"Who's meeting you son," the conductor asked, grabbing hold of my arm to steady me.

I'd paid little attention to him earlier when he punched my ticket. Now I found myself looking up into the eyes of a giant. A thin mustache lined his upper lip and his brown eyes were warm and friendly.

"I'm living with my aunt and uncle for the summer," I said, and then blurted out before I could think, "You're tall!"

"I've been told that. You just now noticed?" I shook my head. "I guess when you saw me I was always bending over. I'm not so big then." He chuckled and pointed out the door.

The end of the train station slid by and the platform rolled into view. A sense of relief and anguish came over me at the same time. I felt relief that I was finally somewhere safe and the anguish of knowing that I might never see my father again. The engineer applied the brakes and the sound of screeching metal and hissing steam echoed off the walls of the train station. Involuntarily I gritted my teeth. I braced myself as the train came to an abrupt stop, grabbing a bar on one wall for support. The conductor pushed in front of me with a small metal footstool in one hand and jumped down on the platform. He swung around, dropped the footstool, easily reached back, grabbed my heavy suitcase as if it was nothing, and set it down.

"Watch your step, son."

I can't explain the feeling I had that night stepping off the train and onto the Bolivar platform. A slight breeze filled my nostrils with the sweet, tangy smell of new mown hay. Although humid, the air smelled fresher in Bolivar than Kansas City. No car exhaust fumes, no smell from the stockyards, or the belching smoke from factories. The station was small with a waiting room in the middle lined with a couple of benches, like church pews. A ticket booth was located on the south side of the station and the north end was dedicated to shipping.

· "Your folks are here to get you," the conductor said gently, nudging me in the back.

I turned and found my Aunt Holly making a beeline out the door of the train station with her arms outstretched. My Uncle John followed.

"Mac!" she screamed.

She scooped me up in her arms and twirled me around like a little kid with her long red hair covering my face. She smelled of Ivory soap and lavender. I clung to her hard, not wanting to let go. There had always been a special bond between Aunt Holly and me. I never knew what it was that brought me to her until I got older. Aunt Holly had the patience to listen. Whatever I'd say to her, she'd calmly listen to me. She'd never tell me what to do like most grownups. She'd ask me questions that made me think. She was tall with milk white skin and long, flowing red hair and blue eyes that could sparkle to make you laugh or shoot daggers at you with pinpoint accuracy. My dad joked to my mother once, when he didn't know I was around, that the first thing you noticed about Aunt Holly was her ample bosom. My mother had slapped his leg and laughed. It was true.

· "All aboard!" the conductor yelled. The engine shot out a white stream of steam and the whistle drowned out all other sounds as the train prepared to move. "You take care, hear?" he called out to me.

I waved over my Aunt Holly's shoulder.

Aunt Holly started to release me but I couldn't let her go. The tears and fears that had been welling up inside me fought for release. I started crying on her shoulder. A soft hand braced the back of my head and she clutched me even tighter. Her cooing words found my ears.

"It's going to be all right, Mac. I just know it is. You're home now. This is going to be your home for a short while. You know we love you."

The engine puffed, metal wheels scraped against the track, and the earth vibrated as the train began to move. My chin rested on Aunt Holly's shoulder and I nodded. I glanced up to see my Uncle John standing quietly with a towel tucked in his arms like he was holding a baby.

My Uncle John was shorter than Aunt Holly, who seemed like a giant among women. Thin and wiry, he farmed and worked for the Missouri Highway Department. It was John who shared his love of books with me. His small, squinty eyes held a sparkle and his thin lips were parted in a grin as he approached. Although only in his forties, his face was weathered from working outside and carried a roadmap of lines and creases.

"Have a good trip?" he asked, as if nothing had happened.

That was my Uncle John. Focus on the moment and forget what you can't do anything about. He and Aunt Holly were perfectly suited for one another. I stopped embracing Aunt Holly, wiped my runny nose with my forearm, and stared inquisitively at the bundle in his arms.

"Yeah, it was okay. What's that wrapped up in a towel?" I asked as I rubbed my wet face with my hands.

John looked down at the bundle. "What makes you think I have something?"

I took another step forward, found the edge of the towel, and flipped it aside. Buried deep in the towel, a small puppy with dark, sad eyes topped with shaggy brown eyebrows looked up at me. My finger scratched under his white-bearded chin. He looked up at me with sleepy eyes and a long, red tongue slid out of his mouth to lick my hand.

"Is this your dog, Uncle John?" I asked.

Aunt Holly wrapped one arm around my shoulders and with the other, pulled the towel away to expose the rest of the scraggliest dog I'd ever seen. He had a mix of coarse brown and black fur and four long legs that stuck out like beanpoles.

"John thought you needed a friend since we live out in the country.

He's three months old."

"You mean he's mine?"

Aunt Holly shook my shoulders. "Well, what do you think?"

My grin must have covered my whole face as I glanced up at her and then back at the puppy.

"I like him."

John pushed the puppy into my arms and I remember how warm and soft he felt as he nuzzled into the crook of my arm. I have always been amazed at the power of a dog in anyone's life. When life is at its bleakest, a dog can bring sunshine like nothing else can.

"What are you going to call your dog?" John asked.

I looked from Uncle John to Aunt Holly and shrugged my shoulders. "I don't know."

John reached out and covered the puppy with the towel.

"Keep him covered so he doesn't pee on you," he chuckled.

Aunt Holly squeezed me tight and gently brushed the hair out of my eyes. "Let's go home."

"Scooter," I said abruptly.

Aunt Holly got an amused look on her face. "What?"

"I'm going to call him Scooter."

"How'd you know it was a boy pup?" John asked. "Did you look?"

"No, I just figured it was a boy."

John had picked up my suitcase and turned to look back at me.

"Where'd you come up with that name?" he asked.

I shrugged, "I don't know. He just scooted up in my arms when I held him."

"Good name," Aunt Holly said as she pushed me toward the car.

3

The night is different in the country. It's quiet - and lonely if you're not used to it. It drops over you like a blanket and you yearn for some small sound like a car driving by or the chatter of a radio. On this night a full moon lit up the sky and bathed everything with a silver tint. Farmhouses were dark when we passed and as far as the eye could see, nothing moved except John's car. Fifteen minutes after leaving the train station, John swung the car into the gravel driveway and I realized that this would be my home for the foreseeable future. A lone light shone in the living room window of the small clapboard house. A large wooden porch spanned the front and was lined with a couple of metal lawn chairs, a rocking chair, and an old wicker sofa. The house was surrounded by large oak and ash that enveloped the house in shadows in spite of the full moon. John stopped the car and turned off the lights.

"We're home," he said.

Piling out of the car, John took my bag in while Aunt Holly explained where I was to sleep.

"You know that John turned half of the back porch into another bedroom. The floor is still the old porch, which is concrete. I wish the front porch was concrete but I guess they built it first. We walled in everything but there is no closet. It has two windows but no screens. I put an old fan in there and there's a place for your clothes. I found an old dresser at a second hand store. The door to your bedroom is off the kitchen, so it's just a hop and a jump to the breakfast table tomorrow."

I grinned as she tousled my hair. Aunt Holly led me through the kitchen to my bedroom. John had already placed my suitcase on the floor.

"It's cooler out here," she said. "If you don't have any questions, I'm going to let you get settled and I'll see you in the morning."

"Good night, Aunt Holly," I said.

I carried Scooter to the bed and gently laid him down with the towel still wrapped around him. His head poked out and his pink tongue licked my hand. I unwrapped the towel and picked him up in both hands. We were face to face. Two soft brown eyes held mine. A wet, pink tongue slithered out of his mouth and licked my nose and for the first time today, I laughed. Aunt Holly walked back to the bedroom door and knocked on the doorframe.

"Oh, I forgot to tell you. There's a box on the other side of the bed for Scooter. "He needs to sleep in there until he's potty trained. If you want, you can brush your teeth in the kitchen sink."

I unsnapped my suitcase and folded it open. Grandma had packed my bag so I had to search for my toothpaste and toothbrush. With Scooter in my arms and clutching my toothbrush and toothpaste in my hands, I proceeded to the kitchen to brush my teeth. Aunt Holly had placed a washrag and glass beside the sink for me. Scooter flopped down on the kitchen counter and watched patiently while I brushed my teeth. I gazed out the window and saw the pond was barely visible from the kitchen window. I could see the moon's reflection on the still water. Maybe I'd go fishing tomorrow, I thought.

I got Scooter tucked in and I climbed in bed. I kicked at the sheet, never quite getting comfortable. Just when I thought that I might go to sleep, an orchestrated chorus of frogs and katydids rushed through the window and kicked me awake. I wondered if this was going to be my prison for the summer. My baseball mitt safely tucked under my pillow, my mind wandered and thought of all the good times I would miss with my friends playing ball, swimming, and hiking in Swope Park. Instead, I'd be lucky to find someone who played catch here in the sticks. A wave of guilt flooded me as I thought of my father lying in a hospital bed, not knowing if he would live or die. I realized I didn't know him that well, only that he rose at four-thirty in the morning and didn't get off his milk route and home until after six o'clock at night. After dinner, he usually had something that needed fixing around the house. The only time I got to talk to him was at the supper table. Usually our conversations were short and about baseball. Since he'd finished some projects, he was making an effort to spend time with me. My mind flashed back to my father lying on the kitchen floor, his mouth open and breathing like a fish out of water.

What would my family do without my father? Projects he'd started on the house were unfinished. Who would change the storm windows in the fall and spring? Who would change the oil in the car and make minor repairs? The list grew longer that night and it made me weary. Just when I thought I was going to sleep, the noise from outside woke me up. I don't know how long I listened to the chirping and croaking but finally, I fell asleep.

4

I awoke to the crackling sound of frying bacon and the smell of fresh biscuits baking in the oven. Hunger pains gnawed at me and my stomach tightened in a knot. I realized I had eaten very little on Sunday since breakfast. Aunt Holly made biscuits every day. They were like silk on the inside and hard and crunchy on the outside. In my mind I already had a large biscuit slathered with butter and peach or strawberry preserves when Scooter whined and scratched at the side of his box. I sat up in bed and looked around the room to get my bearings. I blinked and wiped the sleep out of my eyes. I reached out for Scooter and scratched the top of his head, which only made him scratch more to get out of his box.

Aunt Holly said he couldn't sleep with me until I trained him to go outside. Since he peed on me before we got home last night, she said it was going to take some time. I sat on the edge of the bed and appraised my new home for the summer. There was a small ugly maroon chest that John had found in a junk store. It sat beside the small twin bed. A plain table with an old gooseneck desk lamp on top of it completed the furnishings. There was a window to let the air circulate and a naked light bulb with a pull chain hanging from the middle of the ceiling. Somehow, it didn't feel like home to me.

Perched on the edge of the box, Scooter's tail wagged eighty miles an hour making a rat-a-tat sound when it hit the side. Still in my underwear, I grabbed the towel in the bottom of the box and wrapped it around his trembling body. Holding him at arms length, I rushed through the kitchen just as Aunt Holly had pulled a pan of fresh hot biscuits out of the oven. The smell made me hungrier. Outside in the backyard, I dropped Scooter on the ground like a rock, unwound the towel, and stood him upright. With my hands planted firmly on my hips, I towered over him and firmly commanded, "Pee!"

Scooter promptly sat down and looked up at me with those sad eyes and wagged his tail. I wrapped my hands around his thin, wiry body, and pulled him up on his four legs.

"Pee," I commanded.

Scooter plopped down on his belly and rolled over on his back. His tongue drooped out of one side of his mouth. I rolled him back over and stood him up and he promptly plopped back on his back again. Aunt Holly opened the back door.

"Walk him over by the tool shed," she said.

"Come on, Scooter," I yelled and started walking in my underwear toward the old shed where John kept a little bit of everything.

Scooter chased after me. After he'd gone just a few feet, Scooter stopped and squatted to pee.

"Praise him real good," Aunt Holly shouted.

I knelt down and rubbed Scooter's neck.

"Good boy."

"Why is Scooter a good boy?" John asked, coming around one side of the tool shed with a crooked walking stick in one hand and an old briar pipe clenched between his teeth. A thin trail of smoke leaked from between his lips as he spoke. The other hand pushed an old cotton hat back on his head. He wore his customary tan work pants and an old World War II army shirt frayed at the collar. He grinned as he reached down to pat Scooter on the head.

"Aunt Holly said I should give Scooter praise when he pees."

"I guess she's right. Your Aunt Holly knows all about dogs. Her father raised hunting dogs. They always had ten or twelve running around their place." He chuckled and took the pipe from his mouth. "Her job was to pick ticks off the dogs."

"How come you don't have a dog?" I asked.

John stood up and looked at me with those light blue eyes that twinkled like he knew something you didn't.

"Just don't," he said. "Maybe someday. You better get washed up for breakfast. Holly took off the summer so she could be home with you. She promised to work one last day to train her replacement."

"She's not going to lose her job?"

John smiled and grasped my shoulders with small rough hands. "No, she won't lose her job. It's part-time and her cousin is the county administrator. Her job is safe, but I will lose mine if we don't get moving. I'm off to a late start this morning. I had to count the cattle this morning and I thought I'd lost one."

"What happened?" I asked.

"I've got one that likes to go out on her own. I found her down by the creek. I call her Lady."

"Did you bring her back?"

I saw that twinkle in his eyes.

"What good would it do? She'd just go where she wants to go again."

Aunt Holly stood at the kitchen table when we walked in and pointed toward a large platter with fried eggs on one end, a pile of bacon in the middle, and buttermilk biscuits stacked at the other end. Aunt Holly's kitchen had a warmth that made you feel welcome. The large round table sat in the middle of the kitchen and was covered in a bright tablecloth with colors of red and gold. The cabinets were natural wood with glass doors showing the stacks of white dishes you usually see in small restaurants and diners. There was nothing fancy about her kitchen but it had a coziness that made you feel at home.

"Breakfast is ready, so wash up," Aunt Holly said.

"You use the kitchen sink and I'll go back to the bathroom," John said.

"Wash 'em good," Aunt Holly said.

"You talking to Mac or me?" John asked.

"Both of you," she replied with a smile.

I picked up the yellow bar of lye soap that Aunt Holly made from bacon grease. When you scrubbed with her lye soap you not only felt like you'd washed all the dirt off but the first layer of skin, too. I built up a good lather because Aunt Holly's eyes didn't stray for a minute.

"Have you heard from my mom?" I asked.

"No, honey, I haven't. It costs so much to call, I doubt she'll call us unless there has been a dramatic change."

"Oh."

Aunt Holly heard the disappointment in my voice. She reached up and grabbed a towel for me and laid it across my shoulders.

"No news is good new, Mac," she said softly.

5

After breakfast John left immediately for Springfield and the highway department. Ten minutes later, Aunt Holly and I had climbed into the old Ford pickup to start the five-mile trip into Bolivar. We left Scooter on the back porch with newspapers scattered about on the floor. I agreed to clean up the messes when we got back home this afternoon.

"You okay?" Aunt Holly asked, her hand resting against the starter button on the dash.

"I'm okay."

"It's going to be okay with your dad. If I have time, I'll call your mom and see how he's doing."

I nodded and Holly pushed the starter. The truck coughed a couple of times, the engine stuttered like it wanted to start, and then died. She pulled the choke out a bit and tried it again. The engine backfired and then roared into life. Aunt Holly raised her eyebrows and gave me a satisfied smile. She grimaced as she struggled to push the floor gearshift into reverse. It wobbled back and forth and then there was the grinding of gears and it slipped into reverse.

"I do better with the car," she explained. "The gearshift is on the column instead of the floor."

The truck backed out onto the narrow, red gravel road and we started toward town. The truck bumped and jostled since it had lost its shock absorbers years ago. John used the truck mainly for hauling around the farm. Aunt Holly usually caught a ride to work with a friend every morning. I held on tight to the doorframe and tried not to think of my dad.

Dust flew in the open window and clogged my nose. Aunt Holly gripped the steering wheel firmly as she tried to dodge the largest rocks in the road. We left a plume of swirling red dust in our wake.

"The county hasn't graded this road since last year. Hold on tight," she yelled over the rumble of the truck just as she hit a large rock that sent both of us out of our seats. "I told you to hold on," she laughed.

Aunt Holly's laugh was infectious. It radiated throughout her body and made you feel good. Her creamy white face with the freckles splotched around her button nose made her look younger. Aunt Holly was like a cozy, flannel blanket in winter. She covered you with her warmth.

"I think you need driving lessons!" I shouted.

She threw her head back and the long, red hair seemed to have a life of its own. Flying in the wind and flapping around her face, Aunt Holly appeared so carefree and happy. Catching me off guard, she reached over and pinched me. Without realizing it, I'd put Kansas City and my dad on the shelf and lived the moment.

We approached the bridge over Mile Branch and there was a loud grinding of metal as Aunt Holly shifted into second gear. The truck rumbled and belched as it fought its way up the rocky incline.

"The road gets smoother at the top of the hill," she said, her hands tightly gripping the wobbly steering wheel.

At the top there was a fork in the road. Aunt Holly turned right toward town. A small sandstone house edged the east side of the road; its yard filled with old appliances and rusted farm equipment. A 1938 baby blue Ford sat in the driveway. I caught a glimpse of a boy in his late teens as he got in the car. He shot a menacing look at us as we passed. A younger girl emerged from the back of the car. Our eyes met and she gave me a weak smile. One hand rose up level with her eyes and her fingers wiggled at me. Our eyes had met for that one second and then she was lost in our dust trail. I've learned that sometimes in life you meet someone and there is an instant connection. I didn't understand it at the time but I felt it.

"Who was that?" I asked.

Holly kept her eyes on the road while her arms rolled back and forth as she attempted to keep the old truck going in a straight line. "Who do you mean?"

"There was a boy and a girl back there by that sandstone house. I've never seen them before."

"I don't know. They moved in a couple of months ago. I don't think they're very friendly. John said he found the boy in the lower pasture down by the creek."

"What was he doing?" I asked.

Holly stole a quick look my way.

"Up to no good. He had a fancy slingshot and was shooting at cans on an old log. John thought he was looking at the cattle."

I glanced again over my shoulder but the girl had faded into the distance.

"You mean he wanted to steal one of John's cows?"

"Times change but rustlers of all kinds still seem to be around. There was a case up in Hickory County where a couple went to church early Sunday morning and when they came home, three-fourths of their herd was gone."

"Has John lost any cattle to rustlers?" I asked.

Holly bit her lips as the truck hit a bump that told us we'd left the gravel road for asphalt.

"We haven't lost any cattle yet but I think we'll have to watch our new neighbor. Everett lives over to the West a bit and he saw that boy take down a rabbit with a sling shot."

"Wow! How did he do that?"

"Everett says he has a fancy store-bought slingshot that lets you aim like a rifle. Says he shoots large ball-bearings and rocks with it."

"That's kind of scary," I said.

"Ain't it though."

6

The town square seemed deserted, as if the early summer heat had driven everybody indoors. A couple of cars were parked diagonally in front of the courthouse and another three or four in front of businesses that lined the square. A car slowly approached from the south and half-circled the square before it sped off to the west, continuing on to Osceola, Clinton, or Kansas City. A tarnished green statue of a World War I soldier stood atop a rock base on the northwest corner. A plaque memorialized the names of those who had died. The soldier held a rifle in one hand, a grenade in the other, as he walked through a landscape of barbed wire and timbers. The limestone courthouse, three stories high, was topped by a statue of justice and a large clock. The older men usually gathered there in the mornings to sit on a small retaining wall and smoke cigarettes, wave at passing friends, or just talk. The thin grass by the front steps wore brown patches of tobacco juice and a layer of cigarette butts. Bolivar had a leisurely tempo during the week and wouldn't wake up until Saturday morning when people filled the stores and cars were packed tightly around the square.

Aunt Holly pulled into a parking place on the south side of the courthouse. Two minutes later we stood before a large door with frosted glass and the word Records printed in black. She reached into her purse, located her key, and unlocked the door.

"Well, here we are," she said. "Sally Emerson should be by shortly. She's going to take my place this summer while you're living with John and me. She's a teacher and is always looking for a summer job. She and her husband are saving up to buy a house. It will take me most of the morning to explain what needs to be done. If it takes longer, how about going over to Kelsey's and getting some of his homemade baloney. He makes a fresh batch on Mondays."

"Okay."

I glanced around the musty smelling room. Large, wooden shelves filled with books and small boxes reached to the tall ceiling. A ladder on rollers and attached to a rail in the ceiling let Aunt Holly climb to the top shelves to retrieve records. A wooden counter spanned the width of the room and a small wooden bench offered the public a place to wait. The parsley green paint was old and chipping. Light from a window on the south wall did little to brighten the room. When Aunt Holly flipped a wall switch, four bare ceiling lights did nothing but enhance the shadows.

"Not a very cheerful place," I said.

Aunt Holly chuckled. "That's why I like to be busy."

I walked around the small waiting area and stopped at the wooden bench to read the names people had carved in the armrest while they waited their turn.

"I don't think I'd like working here," I said.

Aunt Holly stepped behind the counter, reached down to pull out a large ledger and plopped it down with a loud smack. "That's because you don't have to buy groceries."

"What's that?" I asked.

"It's the book that records what transaction took place during the day and where the record is filed. This book is for the entire year and then we start over in January."

"You like your job?"

"I like the people. I get to meet a lot of very nice people. John works in Springfield and we have no children, so it keeps me occupied. Anyway, it's only part-time. I only work until noon most of the time. Now, while I'm waiting for Sally, why don't you go over to the North Ward School and see if anyone is playing ball. I see some boys over there at times. It's a little early but you never know. If no one is there you can stop at the doughnut shop and get you a doughnut." Aunt Holly shuffled through her bag until she found a small coin purse and withdrew a dollar bill. "I like chocolate covered."

With Aunt Holly's dollar carefully folded and tucked in my Levis, I left the town square. I'd forgotten my ball glove but I could probably borrow one. My tennis shoes slapped against the weathered granite of the slab sidewalk. Grass sprouted in the cracks. Weeds mixed with wildflowers filled the drainage ditch between the sidewalk and the street. I thought how different this world was from my own. Everything seemed old to me and backward. There were no organized baseball leagues, just a few boys getting together in a field or the schoolyard and choosing sides.

I saw her sitting alone on the swing the moment the school came into view. She looked so small in the deserted playground. Long, dark blonde hair cascaded over part of her face. The swing did not move. Her hands were extended over her head, clutching the chains as her body leaned forward, one bare foot scuffing the naked ground. I couldn't make out her face but I could sense pain in the ridged lines of her posture. I couldn't take my eyes off her. She reminded me of a painting I saw one time on a school trip to the Nelson-Atkins Art Museum - a young woman sitting in a field. She, too, looked alone. As I drew nearer, I realized it was the young girl Aunt Holly and I passed on the way to town.

7

The playground was like a pasture; overgrown grass and small wild flowers stood defiantly in the growing heat. A makeshift pitcher's mound and home plate were visible in a far corner. On the other side, next to the road, two outhouses stood ten feet apart. A crude sign hung above each door indicating gender. The doors stood ajar. As the day grew hotter, I imagined the flies and bees that swarmed around the holes.

Lost in her own thoughts, the girl didn't look up until I drew nearer. When she finally lifted her head, the blonde hair parted to reveal a pale blank face and somber blue eyes. Two puny legs dangled from under the simple cotton dress that hung on her thin body like a blanket. My legs whipped against the tall weeds as I came toward her, but she didn't move except for that one bare foot scuffing the ground. I could see the red-rimmed eyes and the listless full-lipped mouth. She reminded me now of those pictures of young girls liberated from concentration camps in World War II.

She turned a sullen face toward me and said in a quiet, firm voice,

"I saw you this morning in that truck with that woman. Who are you?"

Caught off guard, I took a step backward, swallowed hard, and attempted to speak. A low, gurgling sound slipped through my lips as I grunted, "Mac."

Her eyes narrowed and her body tensed. "What did you say?"

I gulped and tried it again. "My name is Mac."

She looked me up and down for a second before staring straight ahead as if I didn't exist. Her foot began to kick at the ground again. I felt like a complete fool. At fourteen, girls were a complete puzzle to me and that was very evident now. I scratched my head hoping I could think of something clever to say. Snazzy words that might impress her eluded me. I backed up a couple steps, hoping she had forgotten about me, and started to leave.

"You new here?"

I whipped around to see that nothing had changed. She still sat motionless on the swing.

"Yes, yes I am. I'm staying with my aunt and uncle for the summer." I bravely took a step forward rubbing my hands together. "My father is sick so I have to stay until he gets better."

I silently cursed myself for sounding whiney.

"What's wrong with him?" she asked.

"I think he had a heart attack."

"I see," she replied, looking away as if mulling over what I'd said. Her body suddenly straightened and she kicked back with one foot and the swing began to move back and forth. One foot lazily pushed against the ground as her arms tugged at the chains.

"What's your name?" I asked.

She came to a skidding halt and looked at me. I had hoped to see a smile or some other kind of recognition that I really existed: not so. Her eyes appraised me with caution.

"Dory Grace," she said.

I thought for a second. "I don't think I've every heard that name before."

"I 'spect not," she said and commenced swinging again. This time she swung higher and the blonde hair hung down behind her as her feet stretched for the sky.

"It's a pretty name," I said.

Dory Grace didn't smile or acknowledge my comment. I felt foolish and the long pause demoralized me. As I grew older, I never understood why it was so difficult to communicate with girls. When younger, you pulled their hair, stuck out your tongue, and wham--love! Now I had to talk--feel stuff. I felt like a duck out of water and the harder I tried, the further I got from the water. I overheard my mother one time tell a neighbor that girls matured faster than boys. If that were true, I thought, I just as well quit trying but some need inside me kept telling me not to give up.

Suddenly, she broke the silence.

"You ever think about dying?" she asked.

Startled, I answered before I thought.

"That's crazy!"

The swing came to an abrupt halt. Her bare feet dug into the powdered dirt, blowing a cloud of dust into the air. A cold anger iced Dory Grace's somber blue eyes.

"I'm not crazy! Don't tell me you never had thoughts."

I hesitated and considered for a second. "Sometimes...when I've been punished...stupid things fill my head...but that doesn't mean I would really do it."

Dory Grace turned away and started to swing with a renewed vigor.

"Told you so," she said in a short-clipped tone.

"Do you think about dying?" I asked, almost apologetically.

She swung higher now, her thin body lying almost horizontal to the ground. A hard smile broke across her face.

"Sometimes I do," she said matter-of-factly.

"Why would you think that?" I asked.

"Because to die would be freedom," she answered, bringing the swing to an abrupt stop again. This time her feet were completely hidden in dust. She hopped out of the swing and I saw that the melancholy had disappeared, replaced by a sudden exuberance. "Where did you say you come from?" she asked, hands on her hips.

I shook my head in dismay. Dory Grace had gone from a somber, angry, and melancholy girl who talked of dying to the complete opposite in less time than a heartbeat. At that moment, my understanding of girls had reached a new level of misunderstanding. I stood dumbfounded, at a complete loss for what to do or say. I stepped back as she approached me, amazed when she slung one arm through mine to lead me toward the lone teeter-totter.

"I'm from Kansas City," I answered.

 "You gonna move here?"

I shook my head. "No, I'll return to Kansas City when my dad gets better."

She immediately slipped her arm out of mine. "Oh," she said, not hiding the disappointment in her voice.

Somehow, that disappointment gave me courage: a girl might like me.

"I'll probably be here the whole summer. At least that's what my Aunt Holly told me."

Dory Grace strolled ahead of me, her skinny legs almost hidden by the billowing fabric of her dress. She slipped a leg over one end of the teeter-totter. A hand pushed the blue dress between her legs before she plopped down hard on the wood and grasped the handles.

"Get on." A silly grin on her face, she pointed toward the other end. I placed my hands on bare wood smoothed by years of young children's play. "Push it down real hard," she said

My hands gripped the end of the teeter-totter. I pushed and my end crashed into the dust. Skinny Dory Grace shrieked as she flew into the air. My heart jumped into my throat. I stood motionless for a moment as she landed and rolled across the ground, arms flying every which way, and emitting a loud, mournful scream. Once she stopped and sat up with grass in her hair and dust on her face, my feet finally moved.

"I--I didn't mean to do that," I stammered, running to her side. My trembling arms waved around her head not knowing what I should do.

Dory Grace burst out laughing and pointed a taunting finger at me. "I fooled you," she gasped.

I sat back on my haunches and stared at the frail girl who was, for lack of a better word, crazy - but crazy in an exciting way. When she laughed, her eyes danced. You forgot the thin body lost in the oversized dress. I felt a need, a hunger, a yearning in her that I really couldn't comprehend at fourteen-years of age. Like a caged dog, Dory Grace seemed to have broken free for the moment, carousing around the neighborhood looking for adventure. It might have been that she didn't know me, or me her, that allowed her that brief escape into laughter - I didn't know.

"You're crazy," I said, shaking my head. I laid my hand on her shoulder and gently pushed.

Something snapped in her. A spark leaped into her face. Breaking into a large grin, she tucked her knees under in a crouching position and, like a cat, sprang at me.

"Crazy enough to pin a city boy down," she shrieked.

I really didn't know what to do. My parents taught me to never wrestle, hit, or fight with a girl and now I found myself flat on my back as this laughing girl straddled my chest. Her sharp, bony hips dug into my flesh. Her short, rigid fingers snaked their way under my arms and I began to wiggle with laughter. Dory Grace proved to be very skilled at the art of tickling. In desperation, I grabbed her arms and pushed hard until she slid from my body and fell on her back.

"Your turn!" I cried.

My body towered over her and my fingers searched for their mark. Suddenly, a rough hand grabbed me by the scruff of my neck, pulled me into the air, and tossed me to the ground like I was an old dishtowel. Flat on my back, I rubbed my head and wondered what had happened.

I heard Dory Grace scream, and this time the fear was unmistakable.

"Leave me alone, Tony!"

I propped up on one elbow. My blurry vision made out a tall, thin teenager around sixteen or seventeen who had clasped Dory's thin arm in a tight grip and had roughly pulled her to her feet.

"Get back where you belong," he snarled.

"You don't own me, Tony!" she screamed.

Tony's right hand cuffed Dory Grace so hard on the cheek that she stumbled back into the swing. She grabbed the chain to steady herself with a look of disgust on her face.

"Do as you told!"

She snapped, "You ain't got no right, Tony..."

Tony raised his right hand again while the left pointed to the idling car parked in the shade by the outhouses. "Get to the car, Dory!"

"You leave him alone, Tony. He meant no harm."

Mystified by this whole experience, I realized that these people were different from anybody I'd ever met. Who was Dory Grace? Why was Tony hitting Dory? Most important to me now was what was Tony going to do to me? Dory glanced at me for a second before she lowered her head and ran toward the car crying. Tony watched her until she reached the car before he turned his attention to me.

Without a doubt, Tony was the meanest boy I'd ever seen or met in my life. He had long muscular arms on a tall, lean, and tanned body. He wore no shirt and long crisscrossed white scars adorned his chest. His wicked smile exposed jagged teeth that looked like they'd been filed into points. The eyes were the most frightening: small, dark almond eyes that held pure evil. There was no doubt in my mind that Tony loved to hurt people. It emanated in every movement he made, every facial expression. My heart thumped so hard my chest hurt. He took a step toward me and I scrambled backward, pushing hard against the ground with my elbows as he approached. His eyes narrowed and his mouth formed a sinister smirk. I actually feared for my life at that moment. I couldn't get away from Tony's savage kick. His thick army boot hit me in the side and the follow-through rolled me over onto my stomach. Dirt filled my eyes and mouth. I gulped for air. The next kick landed under my armpit and flipped me onto my back again. The last kick clipped my chin and brushed up against my nose. I immediately felt blood spurt down my face. I cried in pain. I cried in fear. My life experiences were void of the bullies like Tony in this world. As he bent over and jabbed a finger into my chest, I felt the sheer terror of the moment. My trembling hands covered my eyes to hide from the fatal blow. A low moan of acceptance slipped from my lips. Tony pried my fingers from my face, bending them backwards until I screamed in pain. He stared at me with pure hatred.

"Don't get near my sister again!" his hoarse voice yelled. "She mine."

His sputum sprayed my face and I smelled acrid tobacco smoke. He jabbed me hard with his fist in the chest, deflating my lungs. In desperation my hands pushed against my chest as I gasped for air. Tony gave me a crooked smile, rose up, and stood astride my body. He worked his mouth as if chewing tobacco. A large blob of spit pushed through and hung tenuously on his lips. I turned my head in disgust as he spit and the wet blob landed on my cheek and rolled down onto my neck. Stepping over my prone body, he calmly started back to his car. I grasped my throat believing that I would never breathe again. I watched Tony climb into the car and as he started to close the door, looked back at me and laughed. I thought I saw Dory Grace chance a look back at me as the car drove away. Alone on the playground, a rush of air finally filled my lungs and I heaved a sigh of relief. The tears started as a trickle and then I began to sob uncontrollably, thankful to be alive.

8

I walked into the Records office where Aunt Holly and Sally Emerson stood talking behind the counter. An elderly woman stood on the other side of the counter listening patiently. Sally Emerson looked up first to see me come in the door. A tall, skinny lady with creamy white skin, her large brown eyes opened as wide as a hoot owl's the minute she saw me. One hand threw her long brown hair behind her shoulder and the other grabbed Aunt Holly's hand. Aunt Holly glanced up at Sally with a puzzled look. Sally nodded toward me standing at the door.

"Mac, what happened to you?"

Aunt Holly rushed around the counter and grabbed me by both arms. Over her shoulder Sally Emerson had turned to the customer and they talked in hushed voices. Aunt Holly eyes scanned my face as if searching for the slightest nick or cut that would lead to instant death. Her hand disappeared inside her blouse and appeared again with a clean, white handkerchief she'd tucked in her bra. A finger wound around the handkerchief and with a quick dip in her mouth to moisten it, she began to rub around my nose.

"Hey, that hurts!" I yelled.

"Sally, call Doctor Jeffers and tell him I'm bringing my nephew over for attention." She looked deep into my eyes and asked, "Who did this?"

Sally nodded and went over to the desk and picked up the phone. Aunt Holly didn't lose a step as she pulled me behind her with me holding her handkerchief to my nose.

"I don't need the doctor," I pleaded.

Aunt Holly grasped my shoulders and stared into my eyes. "Mac, answer me. Who did this to you?"

"I don't know," I whined.

"That's okay, Mac. Let's go see the doctor."

Although we met no people on the way to the doctor's office, my fragile ego felt ashamed to be paraded down the street because I couldn't take care of myself. My protests fell on deaf ears. Doctor Jeffers' office was just south of the square next to the only local bar and across the street from the library. Aunt Holly didn't wait for traffic to pass. She jumped off the curb and held her arm up like a traffic cop and marched across the street dragging me behind her. Doctor Jeffers opened the door for us and led us straight to his office.

"I have John Thomas Olson in the examining room," he explained, "so let's go into my office."

Dr. Jeffers' office was small and painted an ugly cream color. The walls were a thick plaster with swirl designs that didn't look very symmetrical. His cluttered desk sat against the wall opposite the door and an open paper wrapper revealed a half eaten sandwich. The office smells like fried onions. A half-empty bottle of Dr. Pepper sat next to the hamburger.

Doctor Jeffers pointed to an old rickety chair next to the door.

"Sit down there, Mac, and let me have a look."

I sat down heavily on the chair, silently voicing my objection to being examined. Both of his hands grabbed my head and tilted it back. A wayward thumb rested on my nose. He gently pried my nose up to survey the damage.

"Ouch!"

"Hold still, son," Doc Jeffers said quietly.

"I can't breathe," was my muffled response.

"Does he need any stitches?" Aunt Holly asked, her hands nervously brushing imaginary wrinkles out of her skirt.

Doctor Jeffers scrunched his nose to push his glasses up so he could see the damage better. A steady hand grasped my chin and rocked my head back and forth. A short, thin man with light sandy hair, he curled his thin lower lip up over his upper lip and frowned. I waited anxiously for an answer. The thought of some country doctor putting a needle and thread to my face frightened me.

"Nope, I don't think so--unless you want one Mac."

He gave me playful grin with a twinkle in his eye as he patted my shoulder.

"No sir! I don't want any stitches," I grunted through clenched teeth since he still had my chin tightly in his grip.

Doctor Jeffers released me and placed both hands on my shoulders. "I didn't think so. We'll just clean you up a bit. I think you're going to be all right. It looks worse than it really is." He smiled at Aunt Holly to ease her mind. "He bled a lot and that made it look bad. It's pretty much stopped now."

"Who'd you say did this, Mac?" Aunt Holly asked.

I hung my head and stared at my feet.

"That boy we talked about this morning. I don't know his last name. You know, the one with the fancy slingshot. His sister called him Tony,"

I said. "He's the meanest kid I've ever seen and he looks it. His teeth are pointed like... like something you'd see at the show."

"Why? Why did he do this?"

"He didn't want me to play with his sister."

"Why? Were you hurting her?"

"No. I don't know why he didn't want me to play with her." Aunt Holly cocked her head to one side and got a far away look on her face. "That's the truth, Aunt Holly."

Doctor Jeffers raised his eyebrows and glanced at Aunt Holly.

"Was his sister named Dory?" Doctor Jeffers asked, turning around to face Aunt Holly.

I saw Aunt Holly glance at him and an unspoken message passed between them. She nodded her head. Doctor Jeffers continued toward a small cabinet on the wall behind his desk and extracted a bottle of clear liquid. I looked warily at it, hoping it wasn't alcohol.

"Yes," I answered. "He called her Dory and she called him Tony."

Doctor Jeffers opened a glass jar and pulled out some cotton balls. He turned to me with a smile on his face and said, "Let's get you cleaned up." He soaked a cotton ball and dabbed at the blood and the sharp smell of alcohol shot up my nose, and made me pull back involuntarily. "Hold still, Mac." He tossed the bloodied cotton ball in a wastebasket beside his desk and tilted the bottle to wet another cotton ball. "Were there any adults with them, Mac?"

"Ow, that stings!" I shouted.

"Hold still," Dr. Jeffers said calmly.

Aunt Holly repeated the question. "Were any adults around?"

"I don't think so," I replied. "I mean, I didn't see any." I hesitated before adding sheepishly, "She's nice."

Doctor Jeffers started cleaning the rest of my face. "I'd stay clear of those folks," he said, glancing at Aunt Holly and shaking his head.

"How much do I owe you?" Aunt Holly asked.

"I'll send you a bill. I need to get back to John in the other room. He's going to think I forgot about him."

Once out of the doctor's office, Aunt Holly marched to the other side of the square to Kelsey's market where she bought soda crackers, some of Mr. Kelsey's homemade baloney, and a jar of dill pickles. She added a couple of Dr. Peppers from a metal cooler at the checkout. Dr. Pepper was a treat for me. You couldn't find it in Kansas City. Aunt Holly reached into her pocket and brought out a coin purse, carefully counting out the exact change. I carried the sack back to the office where she hung out a closed sign and locked the door. After my encounter with Tony and Dory Grace, I thought I wouldn't have an appetite. Once Aunt Holly unwrapped the butcher paper and the sweet, warm smell of homemade baloney filled the air, I was famished. She spread our lunch on the counter and pointed at a ceramic crock filled with water.

"There are some paper cups by the crock. Get me one for my Dr. Pepper. I don't like drinking out of a bottle."

I got up and realized that my ribs were going to be sore for a while. Doctor Jeffers had given me two aspirin but they did little to kill the sharp pain I felt in my side. I grimaced and one hand clasped the sore ribs as I stood up. Those short steps to the crock to get the paper cup shot pain throughout my entire body. I wanted to scream. I heard the comforting words of Aunt Holly behind me.

"It will get better. Doc Jeffers said I could give you two more aspirin in a couple of hours. It's just going to take a little time."

Lunch was short. Sally Emerson had gone home for lunch and would be back any minute. Aunt Holly talked about Scooter and how John had stocked the new pond with bass and blue gill. Just as I tucked the last piece of baloney in my mouth, Sally Emerson came back to work. Aunt Holly cleaned up and reached into her purse. She pulled out a fifty-cent piece and told me to go across the street for an ice cream.

"I still have the dollar you gave me earlier."

I reached into the watch pocket of my jeans and tugged the dollar bill out. Aunt Holly lifted the dollar from me and slapped the fifty-cent piece into my hand.

"By the time you finish your ice cream and walk around the square, I'll be ready to go home."

9

I burst out the door with the fifty-cent piece clutched tightly in my hand. There was a deep blue cloudless sky overhead and a warm, humid breeze blew out of the Southwest: a lazy, humid Monday afternoon. My life had started anew. I tucked the earlier events aside as I thought of the swirl of vanilla ice cream dipped in hot chocolate: a brown derby!

The ice cream store stood on the northeast corner of the square. The nondescript white building had a sign with a picture of a soft ice cream cone that swirled to a point. There was a small glass window on the front of the building that looked more like a window you'd find in a house. A lanky teenager sat on a stool, his feet planted on top of the serving counter, engrossed in a Superman comic. I stood at the window for a second before he looked up.

"I'd like a brown derby please."

"A what?" he asked. He plopped his feet down on the floor and tossed the comic to one side.

"A brown derby," I said.

He dropped both hands on the counter and leaned forward.

"What's a brown derby my little friend?"

I looked at the menu as he tapped his fingers on the counter.

"I think it's like the brown cow you have on the menu."

"One brown cow coming up."

With a dull expression, he swirled the ice cream into the sugar cone and then dunked it into a small vat of hot chocolate. He quickly pulled it out and wrapped the cone in a napkin and handed it to me without saying a word.

I handed him my fifty-cent's. He had to think a minute before he gave me back my change.

"Thanks."

I carefully bit off the small chocolate swirl on top so I could suck the creamy ice cream out until I heard an empty slurping sound. I had anticipated this moment of satisfaction and a gratified sigh slipped through my lips. I don't know why I turned around to look behind me at that moment. Sometimes you have a feeling that something isn't right with your world. I turned and saw Tony Grace emerge from the side of the ice cream store and march across the street, rolling a flat tire before him. I gulped and backed up into the small window counter of the ice cream store and almost spilt my cone on the sidewalk. I started to run back to the courthouse . I had just reached the curb when I heard my name called.

"Hey! Hey, Mac. Don't you remember me?"

Dory Grace sat in the front seat of the baby blue ford parked on the corner with one wheel resting precariously on a rusted tire jack. I nervously glanced to my right and spotted Tony as he turned into the gravel driveway that led to the DX gas station.

"He ain't gonna be back for some time," she said, following my gaze.

"He ain't got enough money to fix that tire, so he's going to have to do some work in trade."

My whole body sighed with relief. Dory Grace's arms were draped through the open window, her head resting on her bare flesh. She didn't smile but the big blue eyes seemed to beckon me to come closer.

"You sure?" I asked.

She nodded. "I'm sure. We had a flat tire and we got no money." She pointed over her shoulder to the right rear. "We ain't got no spare. It will take them a little while to patch the tube." Her eyes darted to the ice cream I held in my hand. "Is that ice cream you have?"

"Yes. It's called a brown derby--or a brown cow. Soft ice cream dipped in chocolate," I explained.

Her eyes stayed riveted on that ice cream cone like it was a diamond. I looked at the hard chocolate coating that had begun to liquefy and meld into the ice cream melting over the cone. Dribbles of vanilla and chocolate began to run down my hand.

"You want it?" I asked, my hand extended the dripping cone toward her.

She clamored to her knees on the car seat and leaned out the window. The car rocked on the tire jack.

"Bring it closer. Tony won't allow me to get out of the car."

"Why not?" I asked.

I handed her the cone. Dory Grace didn't answer until she'd devoured the cone and splotches of chocolate and ice cream stained the sidewalk. From her chocolate ringed mouth, her tongue eagerly licked the sticky remains on her hands. I watched fascinated. I'd never seen anyone eat an ice cream cone so fast. Her body arched out of the car window with hands extended and she had a look of desperation on her face.

"Tony will kill me if he sees me a mess!"

I pulled the wad of napkins from my pocket and handed them to her. "I'll go get some more," I said.

"Wet me a couple, will ya?" she asked.

The clerk was still reading his Superman comic and didn't look up when I soaked the napkins in the water fountain. I hurried back to the car and handed them to her. Dory scrubbed her face hard and the chocolate disappeared, as did the gray tone of her skin that I'd noticed earlier. Her skin was now pink and the blue eyes seemed to sparkle in celebration.

"Thanks, Mac," she said, handing me the wad of wet napkins.

I glanced around to see if anyone was looking before I tossed the wet mess under the car.

"It's okay," I said. "Aren't you hot in that car?"

The car wobbled precariously again as Dory slipped out the window to perch on the frame, looking cautiously in the direction of the DX station.

"This way I can see him when he comes back," she said.

Her arms were tucked inside the car and clutched the roof for balance.

"Why don't you come outside? We can sit over there in the shade." I pointed to the back of the ice cream store, which was shaded by the taller brick building next door.

"I can't. Tony tol' me to stay in the car. I'm fine, thank you."

I rested my hand against the car. The metal was hot. I wiggled around until I felt comfortable. Shading my eyes from the sun with my other hand, I looked at Dory Grace hanging out of the car window.

"Why does Tony say you can't come out of the car? It's hot in there."

Dory laughed and kicked her legs inside the car. Her smile exposed yellowed teeth and I suddenly realized her hair hadn't been washed for sometime. It hung limply down her back. Dory Grace was the exact opposite of any girl I'd known in Kansas City but none had ever held the attraction I felt toward her. There was something about Dory that said

I had to be her friend. I truly didn't understand our bond. I just knew it had to be.

"Tony don't want my spirit to be free because he has no spirit."

I frowned.

"You're strange."

She giggled. "I know. I bet you never met anyone like me before."

"What do you mean about your spirit? Why doesn't he..." I paused and shook my head.

Dory's skinny finger reached out and touched my nose.

"Magic's inside my body and Tony is afraid it will get out."

"Magic?" I asked.

Her eyes became serious and searched beyond me as if something were in the sky. One hand fingered a small string hanging around her neck.

"Everyone has magic if they search hard enough," she said. "Most folks don't see it. Tony don't want my magic to get out because then I'd get away."

"You mean like Houdini or Blackstone?" I asked. Dory seemed puzzled by the question. "The famous magicians," I explained.

She shook her head no and kicked her legs and let out a shrill, "No!"

I sighed and one hand brushed through my hair in frustration.

"I'm lost," I said.

Her forefinger snuck out again and gently touched my chest.

"What you are inside. Each of us is special in our own way. Some people have love and want to do good things. Others only have hate and meanness inside."

"Like Tony?" I ventured.

"Yes, like Tony," she whispered.

I stared at her eyes, those ever changing eyes that now were filled with love. The love wasn't for me but everything around her.

"How old did you say you were?" I asked.

"I'll be fifteen this October."

I was flabbergasted.

"How can you be almost fifteen? You look like you're younger than me," I said.

Dory gave me a smug look and with her arms outstretched, leaned out the car window.

"It's my magic."

Her eyelids fluttered and she swooned and blew a kiss at me like Marilyn Monroe. It was my turn to laugh. Her infectious air made you wonder why anyone would want to stifle her "magic". Her contagious personality drew you in and wouldn't let go.

"I guess I don't know what my magic is," I said.

Dory set up straight with a serious look on her face. "You're a good and honest person, Mac."

I squirmed and shoved my hands in my pocket.

"How do you know that? You don't even know me," I replied.

One hand slipped through the string around her neck and her nimble fingers began to move back and forth like a spider.

"Your magic shows," she said quietly.

Embarrassed, I decided to change the subject.

"My brother tried to teach me how to make Jacob's ladder with string but my fingers don't move right."

Dory pulled the string from around her neck and as I watched in amazement, she formed Jacob's ladder with little effort.

"I learned how to do this 'cause I get bored at home sometimes," she said.

I marveled at the string art and how just as quickly it returned to a simple piece of string.

"That's neat," I said. "Can you teach me?"

. Dory spread her hands apart, stretching the string taunt, and looked at me with a big smile on her face. I could see her magic. I could overlook all the imperfections in her dress, her hygiene, because of her magic.

"Sure," she said. "Get closer and put out your hands."

She started to place the weathered string around my hands when she suddenly pulled back to look behind her. I could see the tension in her body as she flopped back into the car. She didn't have to say anything: I knew. Tony's head bobbed up and down as he pushed the repaired tire back up the hill toward the square.

"Go!" she pleaded.

I turned and ran as hard as I could and hoped that Tony would not see me. As I crossed to the other side of the street by the picture show and ran north up Springfield Street, I thought I heard Dory call after me.

"I'll see you later, Mac."

10

We left the courthouse around three o'clock. I climbed in the truck and looked at Aunt Holly. She glanced my way but didn't say anything. I couldn't tell if she was mad or just aggravated with me. The truck roared to a start and she muttered as she worked to get the gearshift into reverse. There was a loud crunching of metal and she gave me that look that said I'd better not say anything. We were quiet almost all the way home. As we approached the turn-off for the bridge over Mile Branch, we slowed down and I found myself looking at Dory's house. Tall weeds grew waist high in the front yard and it looked like the grass had never been cut. A scrawny cat watched us from his place on top of a rusted milk can. My eyes searched for a sign of the car or Dory.

"That place is a mess," she said.

I had to nod in agreement. The truck started to descend the hill, bouncing over large craters in the road. Aunt Holly didn't say anything. She held the steering wheel tightly in her hands and looked straight ahead. The house came into view and Aunt Holly gunned the old truck until we reached the driveway.

"Home again," she said as she turned off the engine. For the first time since I rushed into the courthouse, Aunt Holly smiled at me. Her blue eyes were sad and teary. "I'm glad you're okay."

Her hand clasped my shoulder and gave me a playful squeeze.

"Me, too," I said.

I smiled at her and remembered something my dad once said to my mother. "My sister is such a hugger. I've never seen anyone hug so much. She even hugged our mother in her coffin." It was true. Aunt Holly was a hugger. In some ways, Aunt Holly reminded me of Dory. She had a certain magic about her.

"Are you going to tell John about what happened?" I asked.

Aunt Holly turned her head away from me and searched the far horizon. I held my breath. I knew John would be mad but the thought of not seeing Dory again bothered me. It also bothered me that I cared. Dory was what my mother would call a rag-a-muffin with her oily hair and soiled grey-colored skin. Dory's appeal to me wasn't physical. She had magic and I couldn't resist that magic.

The remainder of the afternoon I played with Scooter in the front of the house and tried to take my mind off Dory and Tony. Aunt Holly had retreated to the kitchen to prepare supper. I saw the plumes of dust rising into the air before I saw John's car. He pulled into the gravel drive and parked the old Chevrolet next to the Ford pick-up. Holly had told me that she would tell John and for me not to worry. Scooter hopped and barked as John got out of the car. John reached down and scratched behind Scooter's ears. He smiled at me and started walking toward the house.

"You have a good time today?" he asked.

"Uh-huh," I replied, dragging my toe in the dirt.

"I'm going inside and get ready for supper. You better bring Scooter in and wash up.

I followed John into the house. He tossed his fedora on a hat rack by the front door. Aunt Holly came out of the kitchen to greet him. I held my breath.

"Supper is ready. You two better wash up," she said, gently brushing John's cheek with her lips. "So, how was your day?" Aunt Holly asked when we'd taken our places at the kitchen table.

John held a knife and fork in his hands and carefully pushed the pork chop around his plate until he positioned it just right. He sliced off a small piece of meat.

"Okay," he said with a shrug of his shoulders. "Did you get Sally trained?"

"Uh-huh."

"Is she going to work out?"

Aunt Holly thought for a second. "I think so. She's a pretty sharp cookie. I think she's a good school teacher."

"Good," John said, and then to me. "How was your day, Mac? Did you keep busy while Holly trained Sally Emerson?"

I looked up, a large bite of pork chop and boiled potato in my mouth. "Uh-huh."

Thankfully John never talked much during supper and the subject was dropped. From time to time my eyes would stray to Aunt Holly. She'd smile and nod her head, meaning the time wasn't right. After I finished supper, Aunt Holy excused me from the table early. I left them at the table and Scooter and I went to my room. Scooter nuzzled up next to me while I read a Hardy Boys mystery. John and Aunt Holly talked quietly at the dining room table and I could tell that John had become upset. Aunt Holly talked to him in a soothing voice and finally calmed him down.

John came by my room while Aunt Holly washed the dishes. I lay on the bed, my head propped on the pillow while Scooter draped himself across my chest. Scooter raised his head. His tail wagged a hundred miles an hour and he scooted down my chest and onto the bed when John entered the bedroom.

John held his hand out and Scooter licked it. John laughed and playfully scratched the top of Scooter's head before he sat down on the edge of the bed. I put my book aside and sat up. John picked up Scooter and placed him back on my lap.

"He doesn't have a care."

"I don't think so," I said.

John scratched Scooter behind the ear, straightened and cleared his throat.

"Your Aunt Holly told me what happened today. Are you okay?"

"Yeah," I answered, nodding my head. "My ribs are a little sore but not too bad."

"I want you to know that I'm mad as a hornet about this but your Aunt Holly says we should let it go for now. What do you think?"

I looked from Scooter to John. First, I wanted John to go over to Tony's house and beat the tar out of him. Aunt Holly saying 'let it go' hurt me. Second, John was making me part of the decision process and that took me by surprise.

"Well, he beat me pretty bad," I said.

"Where did he get you?"

I raised my shirt and exposed the light red bruise near my ribs where Tony had kicked me. I turned around to show him another bruise on my back.

"Anything else?" John asked.

"He got my nose," I said, pulling down my shirt. "At first I thought he'd ripped it off my face but Doctor Jeffers said he just bloodied it."

"I know you were scared out of your wits. I certainly would have been."

"It happened so fast," I said.

"Don't go near this guy again, understand? I'll take care of this in my own way and time."

11

Tuesday morning I awoke again to Scooter clawing at the sides of the cardboard box. His cries were more urgent this morning. The minute he saw me roll over and look down at him, he pawed harder and began to whine with an urgency that only meant one thing. Picking him up in my arms, I held him to my chest and ran for the back door. Once I reached the backyard, a warm wetness crawled down my chest as Scooter licked at my face.

"Aw, Scooter," I said, holding him now at arms length. "Why did you have to pee on me?"

Scooter showed no concern for my predicament. He wiggled in my hands for me to let him down. I dropped him harder than I should have but Scooter didn't seem to mind. He bounced right back and laid his front paws on my leg. I held the tee shirt away from my chest and carefully tried to ease it over my head. There I stood behind my Uncle John's house in my underwear, tugging a pee soaked tee shirt over my head when I heard a noise and something came to rest against my foot. Goggle-eyed, my arms stretched over my head, I scanned the woods in front of me. I saw nothing. On the ground lay a rock with a folded piece of paper tied to it. I popped the tee shirt off my head and tossed it to the ground. Carefully searching the woods to see who threw the rock, I reached down and picked it up. A rubber band held paper that was yellow with age and dirty. I pulled the rubber band off and found a grocery list. I turned it over and found a note to me in scribbled handwriting.

After you get dressed, meet me at the old schoolhouse.

Thinking it was Tony that wrote the note, a cold chill shot through me until I realized that it had to be Dory. Tony wouldn't take the time to write me a note to meet him. His kind would walk out of the woods and beat me to a pulp. I suddenly became very self-conscious, standing almost naked in the backyard. I reached down to pick up Scooter but he shot off toward the front of the house. There was nothing to do but follow. Scooter wiggled and turned as he attempted to avoid my outstretched arms. Just as I caught him, I looked up to see my Uncle John picking up the morning paper. He stopped to stare at me with Scooter squealing in my arms and started to laugh.

"I think you better go inside before some old lady comes by and you scare her out of her wits."

I ran into the house and found Aunt Holly in the kitchen.

"Your Uncle John needs the bathroom to get ready for work. You wash up in here."

The wash pan sat on a small table beside the icebox. Aunt Holly had a warm kettle of water on the stove and brought it over to the large aluminum pan and filled it. She took the tee shirt from me and made a face.

"I hope this was Scooter's doings," she said smiling.

"He peed on me before I could get him outside."

"Some dogs just don't have any manners," she chuckled and walked toward the back porch and the dirty clothesbasket.

The warm water felt good and I scrubbed my chest especially hard. In no time I was clean and dressed. Breakfast consisted of eggs, bacon, and biscuits and honey. As I washed the last bite down with a glass of raw milk, Aunt Holly rested her arms on the table. Her blue eyes twinkled in the morning light.

"So, what are your plans for this morning?"

I wiped my mouth with the back of my hand and settle back in my chair.

"I don't know. Maybe take a walk through the woods with Scooter toward the old schoolhouse. I haven't been over there in a long time."

"That doesn't sound like much fun," she said.

Uncle John carefully folded the cloth napkin and laid it beside his plate.

"I need to get going," he said. "The fishing poles are in the tool shed if you decide to go fishing in the pond. Just remember not to fish off the dock because the water is over ten feet deep."

"I can swim," I said.

"I know you can," he replied. "I have a flat bottom boat tied up there, too. Maybe this weekend we'll get in it and fish in the middle of the pond. Be careful. Sometimes things happen when we don't want them to."

"Okay," I said.

John got up from the table and headed back to the bathroom to finish getting ready for work. Holly folded her hands in front of her and bent forward to look in my eyes.

"I think I have a plan for this morning. I think I'll wash the dishes and do some laundry and then maybe we can go fishing together. How would that be? It'll take me about two hours to finish the laundry and hang it out. It's seven now, so let's say we go around ten. That will give me time to hang the clothes on the line."

"That would be great!"

Aunt Holly laid one hand on top of mine.

"I called your mom this morning," she said.

I sat there for a second, taking a deep breath that filled my lungs. My arms wrapped around my chest as I prepared for the bad news. A thin smile crept across her face.

"Your father had a stroke, not a heart attack," she said.

"Is he going to be okay?" I asked meekly.

"The doctors think so. Only time will tell."

"When will they know?"

"All I know is that he's resting and your mom is hopeful. We'll know more later."

"Then he's awake?"

"I guess so. Like I said, your mom sounded hopeful."

"Does that mean I can go back home?" I asked.

Aunt Holly laughed.

"No, I'm afraid not. I think you're stuck with your Aunt Holly for the summer." Aunt Holly reached over and pinched my cheek before pushing her chair back and picking up our breakfast plates. "Now go brush your teeth and get walking. And remember to check Scooter for ticks when you come back home. The woods are filled with them this time of year."

I had to wait for John to finish in the bathroom before I could brush my teeth. Aunt Holly bought Pepsodent toothpaste, my favorite. I was curious about the note. Why did Dory throw a rock at me with a note tied to it? Why didn't she just call or come to the door and ask if I was home? The mystery of it all excited me. It reminded me of something that would happen in a Hardy Boys mystery.

The one-room schoolhouse sat just west of John's property. At one time, most of the kids living north of Bolivar had gone to school there. After World War II the population started to shift to Bolivar and the schoolhouse had fewer students. It didn't look like any school that I'd ever seen. Desks faced the south and the teacher's desk faced west. The east side of the schoolhouse was filled with tall windows and during a sunny day, it was as bright as outside. A large blackboard almost covered the entire west wall. It was hard to believe that a school smaller than my classroom in Kansas City housed students from first through eighth grade. Whenever my parents came to visit, John and my mom would always take a walk by the old schoolhouse and relive ancient memories. I wondered what memories they could have that were so wonderful. There was no asphalt playground, no circles for dodge ball or bases for kickball. The bathrooms looked worse than the ones I saw yesterday in the North Ward schoolyard. It's puzzled me how grownups could think this old building held pleasant memories.

I walked the narrow cow path through the woods of tall, skinny oak trees with Scooter snuggled in my arms and occasionally I dodged a fresh cow paddy. It was only around seven-thirty and I could tell it was going to be another muggy day. Heat in the middle of a wooded area is different than heat in the city. There is no concrete or asphalt to contain the heat in the country. As I drew nearer the schoolhouse, I felt an excitement I had never experienced before. Was this love? Was I falling in love? I know I never had feelings like this before. My heart pounded and my breathing was rapid and short. Emerging into a small clearing, the road that ran in front of John's house became visible to my right. Directly ahead sat the schoolhouse with its weatherworn clapboard siding and faded red-shingled roof. A wooden black window screen had come loose and hung precariously from one window. A large bell stood atop a thick, wooden pole by the backdoor and there, on the small, concrete stoop, sat Dory in her familiar pose; arms wrapped around her legs and her chin resting on her knees. She didn't move when she saw me but I could see the gleam in her eye as I walked toward her. The blond curls framed a face that looked different today and then I realized she washed her face and hair.

"Hi," I said, standing in front of her.

"Hi yourself," she replied, her voice low, almost playful.

"What did you want?" I asked.

Dory started to giggle.

"You always go outside in the morning in your shorts? You gave everybody north of Bolivar an eye-full."

She buried her face in her arms and laughed so hard her whole body shook.

"What were you doing looking at people so early in the morning." I said.

She looked up at me with tears of laughter in her eyes. "You could say I saw you naked."

"You did not!"

"You sure didn't leave much to my 'magination," she chortled.

I started to become angry. My foot scuffed at the hard, red clay and I looked around to make sure we were alone.

"Scooter had to go to the bathroom!" I said, nodding at the struggling Scooter in my arms.

"Looks like he needs to go again," she said. One hand reached up to pet him on top of the head. "You going to take your clothes off again?"

"Don't be stupid!" I shouted.

Scooter tumbled out of my arms and Dory grabbed him by the scuff of the neck. She brought him up to her face and nuzzled him with her nose. Scooter hung like a limp rag in her hands and his little tongue meekly reached out and licked her.

"He wants to be free," she whispered.

"Why would you say that? He is free," I said.

Dory's hollow blue eyes looked past me. Her mind was far away and when she spoke, her voice was quiet and distant.

"Because we all want to be free."

Suddenly, she came back from wherever she'd gone and gave me a fleeting smile as she sat Scooter on the ground. His short puppy legs wobbled and he fell flat on his face. Dory stroked his head as struggled to his feet.

"I don't want to be free," I said unconsciously. "At least not yet. I still have to grow up."

"You are free, you just don't know it," she answered in that melancholy voice.

Dory stood up and for the first time I realized she didn't have on any shoes. She wore an old pair of oversized jeans and a white tee shirt that revealed budding breasts through the thin material.

"What did you want?" I asked.

"To see you," she answered.

It was hard for me to understand a girl with Dory's directness. In my limited studies of girls, I found her directness a complete mystery. Dory was not of this world.

"Why did you want to see me?"

"Because I like you, silly," she said, taking one long finger and running it down the bridge of my nose.

Those strange feelings crept back into my body and I felt an excitement I really didn't know how to control. The skin on the back of my neck tingled. My heart started beating so hard that I could hear it. How could this girl, one year my senior, like me? How did she like me? As a friend? Boyfriend? I found myself completely bedazzled and befuddled at the same time.

"I don't understand," I said.

"For someone from the city, you sure don't know much," she replied. She grabbed my hand and pulled on it. "Grab Scooter. I want to show you my secret place."

12

With Scooter bundled in my arms, I followed Dory. She led me on a cow path through a band of trees between two fields and headed south toward Mile Branch. I knew where I was but I'd never been this way before. Dory walked unbothered by the rocks, gnarled roots, and clumps of brush. She reminded me of a firewalker crossing a bed of hot coals. Every once in a while she stopped, listened carefully, and then waved at me to follow. I started to say something to her but was immediately shushed by a warning look and a quick hand over my mouth. My father had talked about mood swings in women with a friend of his one time and Dory's actions made me wonder if this is what he meant. I kept quiet and passively follow her lead. To my left the pasture gave way to a field of newly planted corn. Tender sprouts, two feet high, waved in the breeze as we passed. John had planted feeder corn in May for the cattle and I wondered if it would make it through a hot, dry summer. I heard the creek ahead as it ran shallow across bedrock. The sound made me thirsty. We left the field and entered the tree line that bordered the creek. The trees were thicker and lush, while green foliage and vines covered the ground.

"Poison ivy," Dory mouthed as we wound carefully around the three-pointed leaves and made our way down to the creek bank.

A tranquil pool lay before us and at one end, the water calmly cascaded over a natural formation of rocks that spanned the creek. I held Scooter to my chest as we stepped across this natural dam and continued up the bank on the other side. Following another cow path through the trees, we moved steadily away from John's farm and the road that ran by Dory's house.

"Why didn't we cut across the pasture instead of going through the trees? It would have been faster," I said.

Dory turned and placed her hands on her hips. With tight lips, she nodded her head and cast her eyes to the ground. We froze in time for a moment and I nervously shifted from one foot to another while I waited for an answer. I didn't understand why we were being so secretive and quiet.

"Because, it wouldn't be a secret place," she whispered, and turned, leading us farther away from the farm.

A short time later we started climbing a small hill. Dory turned sharply to her left. I glanced up to see a large white oak spreading across the sky and towering over the small saplings surrounding it. The small oaks were so crowded that none of them would ever become strong, mature trees. As I slipped through this miniature forest, I saw a small lean-to. Thin branches had been strung together with twine and leaned against a low-lying limb of the white oak. A large, five-gallon lard can sat in the middle of the lean-to. Dory opened it and pulled out an old rug someone had made out of scraps of cloth. She carefully spread it on the ground.

"Have a seat," she said, gesturing toward the rug.

I sat cross-legged on the rug and marveled at the secrecy of this place. Someone could pass ten feet away and if they weren't looking, never see us. Eyes closed, her head titled upward, Dory sat beside me with a serene expression. I can see her today as vividly as I did over fifty years ago. Time cannot erase those memories etched in your brain. I'd never seen Dory so calm, so peaceful, as when she took me to this special place. I realized then that whatever ghosts haunted her soul that they were not allowed to enter this sacred place.

"Can't you feel it?" she whispered.

"Feel what?" I asked.

She opened one eye and looked at me in disbelief.

"The specialness of this place."

Since my mother had been an English major in college before she married my dad, and corrected my grammar every chance she got, I questioned in my mind if specialness was a real word. It didn't matter, because I understood what she meant. Although I liked her secret place, what really made it special were the feelings Dory had for it and that she shared those feelings with me.

"Yes, I really like it."

"You do?" she asked. Her voice had become soft.

"Yep. I really like it."

Dory reached behind her to pull out a dirty canvas bag, the type I'd seen in Army surplus stores. She unfolded the bag and pulled out a simple Big Chief tablet and held it up between us. Her blue eyes hardened and a determined expression replaced the serenity.

"This is my life. My story. When I die, I want you to show the world."

"What do you mean when you die? You're not going to die. You're fifteen years old and have a long life ahead of you."

"Promise me!" she said, gritting her teeth.

I couldn't return her gaze, so I dropped my eyes to the ground and nodded.

"Say it," she said.

"I promise," I mumbled.

"Good," she said, and replaced the tablet in the canvas bag. Once the bag was back in the lard can, she closed the lid and turned to me with a bright smile on her face.

"Come on. I want to show you something."

She took my hand and led me from the lean-to.

"Look over there to your right," she instructed.

We had traveled a short distance to where we stood above the lean-to under the canopy of the giant white oak. I moved my eyes over the tops of the trees that lined the creek. I saw the large pond below John's house, the raw, darkened limestone bluff immediately behind the pond, and John's barn. I stood on tiptoe and could see through the band of cedars that lined the back of John's property and found the tool shed that stood directly behind the house.

"I can see the tool shed but not the house," I said.

"Sometimes when I'm up here, I see your Aunt Holly get in the boat and go to the center of the pond to fish."

"You come here often," I asked. She answered with a shrug and dull eyes. "Who else knows about this?" I asked, my arm sweeping toward the lean-to below.

"Just you--and another friend. He won't never tell."

Her voice was a whisper and her eyes pleaded to keep this secret.

"Who else knows?" I asked.

"It don't matter. Just know that he won't tell."

"I won't tell," I replied. My hand reached out to touch her shoulder.

She nodded and started back down toward the creek.

"We'd better go. Tony will get home soon and I don't want to be caught not bein' there."

"Why does Tony watch over you so much?" I asked.

"He thinks he owns me," she answered without turning around.

I stumbled behind Dory as if I was the one who had no shoes. Her arms swung freely and a hand trailed against the tall grass that grew next to the cow path.

"What will happen to you if he finds out you're gone?"

She didn't answer.

13

I walked into the yard with Scooter in my arms to find Aunt Holly standing by the clothesline with a basket of wet clothes. Clothespins were stuck in her mouth as she wrangled with a white sheet that didn't want to cooperate. I put Scooter down and he immediately took after a small moth flittering in the air.

"Hi, Aunt Holly."

She gave me a curt nod and continued wrestling with the sheet.

"Something wrong, Aunt Holly?"

Aunt Holly turned and spat the clothespins out of her mouth into a small shoebox on the ground. Her fists doubled, she placed them on her hips and bent over until our noses almost touched. Her blue eyes were cold and hard. Her lips formed a fine line and she pinched them together so hard they were void of color. I arched backwards but her nose followed.

"Where have you been?" she asked.

Her hot breath blew across my face and I found myself struggling for air.

"I met Dory at the old schoolhouse and we went for a walk," I answered in a hushed voice.

"Why didn't you tell me?"

Aunt Holly straightened and her hands fell to her side but her face was still stone cold.

"I--I don't know."

"Don't give me that, Mac. Why didn't you tell me?"

"You wouldn't approve," I muttered.

"You don't know if you don't ask," she said.

"I'm sorry."

"Don't you sorry me. The second morning you're here, I find you go gallivanting with the sister of the guy that beat you up. I'm beginning to wonder if you have your head screwed on straight."

Aunt Holly picked up a couple of clothespins and returned to the wayward sheet.

"I'm sorry, Aunt Holly, but I like her. She's nice."

"Help me with this sheet. My friend, Irma, gave me this new-fangled fitted sheet and I'll be damned if I can get it on the line. Just hold that end until I can figure out how to do this."

"I won't do it again," I said. "I'll tell you. Don't be mad at me."

Aunt Holly gave an exasperated sigh as she finally got one end pinned. She brushed the sheet with her hand as she pinned it in the middle and then the other end.

"Won't do what again?" she asked.

"I'll be sure and tell you where I'm going."

Aunt Holly turned and picked up the basket and walked toward the house. "You better start thinking about how you're going to get those fleas off of Scooter before he comes in the house." As she opened the screen door to the back porch, she stopped and glanced back at me. "This is your one chance. Don't do it again."

I had never seen Aunt Holly mad before. From the moment I met her, she had been one of the happiest, easy-going people I'd ever met. There was another side to Aunt Holly that I met that day and I didn't want to meet her again.

I gave Scooter his first bath. I don't know who was wetter when we finished. After he'd dried off, Aunt Holly gave him a dog biscuit of barley, flour, salt, baking soda, and a touch of garlic. She told me I was to give him one three times a day: no more, no less. I'd have to check him every night for ticks and pick them off. The biscuit smelled horrible but Scooter attacked it like it was the best treat in the world. By the time he'd finished it was time for lunch. Holly made fried country ham sandwiches with potato chips and a glass of milk. There is nothing as good in this world as sugar cured ham. One of the neighbors had given Aunt Holly the ham for some sewing she'd done for them. Thick slices of ham coated with mayonnaise and horseradish and chased with raw milk was a great treat when my family visited Bolivar. We ate in silence. I did not want to aggravate Aunt Holly. I finished and pushed my plate away, held my belly, and gave a big groan.

"You full?" she asked.

"I'm more than full," I said, patting my stomach.

"You want to take a nap?"

I made a face.

"I don't want to do that! That's for little kids."

"You're not tired?"

I gave Aunt Holly a puzzled look.

"Why would I be tired?"

"Well, you were moaning and groaning after you ate. I was going to ask you if you and me could take our fishing poles and see if we could catch some catfish for dinner. Maybe even make a jar of lemonade to take along if we got thirsty."

I jumped up from the table and took my plate to the sink.

"Can I take Scooter?" I asked.

"I wouldn't if I were you. We don't want him falling in the water," she said, reaching for an empty ball jar in the cabinet over the sink. "Anyway, you don't want to give him another bath so soon. Put him in the box by your bed and I'll make the lemonade. After you get him in the box, you go wait for me on the front porch."

Aunt Holly already had the tackle box, bait, and poles leaning against the side of the house. Five minutes later she came bursting out the front door with a big smile on her face.

"You ready?" asked. She tossed one of John's old St. Louis Cardinals baseball caps at me. "Put this on to keep the sun out of your face."

I crammed the hat on my head and bent down to pick up the fishing poles.

Aunt Holly wore an old straw hat that use to belong to her father. The brim was frayed and the holes from age competed with the natural holes from the weave. She always wore it when we went fishing. She said it brought her luck. One time I asked her if she could still smell her dad on the hat. A silly smile spread across her face, exposing her pearly white teeth. A hand rubbed the top of my head but she never answered me.

"I'm ready," I answered. "I see you have your fishing hat."

"I just can't let go of it," she said as she pushed it down on her head. "I feel my daddy when I put it on."

We'd just left the porch and started for the pond when the Grace's old baby blue Ford pulled in the driveway. The car belched blue smoke as Tony accelerated toward the house. There was someone in the car with him in the passenger's seat. Someone I didn't recognize. I saw the top of Dory's head in the backseat. The car stopped with a savage lurch directly in front of us. Aunt Holly dropped her fishing pole, grabbed my arm and pulled me behind her. She held me close as a woman got out of the car on the passenger's side and walked briskly toward us. I couldn't guess her age but her face was hard with deep lines and wrinkles that made a crisscross pattern. Her straight hair hung limply to her shoulders. She wore a simple cotton dress that resembled a gunnysack in color and style. She stopped abruptly and pointed a short, bony finger at me.

"Is this 'un yours?" she asked, staring straight ahead at Aunt Holly.

Aunt Holly's body stiffened, her jaw taut, as her hand gripped my arm tighter. It seemed like forever before anyone spoke. I snuck a nervous glance toward Tony. He seemed more interested in cleaning his fingernails with a toothpick than watching what was unfolding outside the car.

Finally, Aunt Holly spoke in a flat, lifeless voice.

"I beg your pardon?"

The face-off continued. I could tell Mrs. Grace did not like Aunt Holly--or me. Her eyes were a lifeless gray and stone cold. Yellow, tobacco stained teeth bit at dried, cracked lips as if she were assessing Aunt Holly. The hands clenched at her side, she took a deep breath and her nostrils flared like a horse after galloping.

"I'm Harriett Grace. I live up on the hill in the sandstone house. That girl in the car is my step-daughter, Dory."

Aunt Holly's eyes did not leave Mrs. Grace. I stole a glance at the car and found Dory's head bent over with her hands over her ears. Tony looked up at me and smiled. My eyes shot back down to my feet.

"I'm Holly McReynolds and this is my nephew, Mac."

"I want him to stay away from my step-daughter," she said, brusquely pointing a knobby finger in my direction. The nails were jagged down to the quick and etched with grime.

"I'm sorry?" Aunt Holly inquired coldly.

Mrs. Grace's eyebrow shot up and her jaw tensed.

"I think you heard me."

Aunt Holly stood up straight and let go of me. She defiantly crammed her hands against her hips and threw her head back. "Maybe your step-daughter should stay away from my nephew," she said sharply.

I don't know if Mrs. Grace was used to someone like Aunt Holly because she took a step back. Her eyes narrowed, as she looked Aunt Holly up and down with a new appreciation. Biting at her lower lip and staring at Aunt Holly with the most hateful look anyone could muster, Mrs. Grace turned to look at Tony and then back at Aunt Holly.

"If that boy gets near my step-daughter, my boy knows what to do."

Aunt Holly's right hand flew from her hip and rested directly under Mrs. Grace's nose. I shot a glance at Tony who had started to open the door. Aunt Holly's other hand reached into her jean pocket, pulled out a knife, and flipped the blade open so fast it startled me. I'd seen the knife before. It was the one that Aunt Holly took when we fished.

"If he lays one finger on Mac, I'll cut his balls off and nail them to your front door. Do you understand?"

Aunt Holly's voice was cold and brittle. Tony's hand rested on the doorframe waiting for his mother to say something. Mrs. Grace cast her eyes to the ground and her head began to visibly shake. I don't know whether it was from anger or fear. Suddenly she raised her head, shot a parting glance at Aunt Holly.

"You heard what I said."

She walked back to the old car and motioned for Tony to start it up. They were leaving. Aunt Holly stood in the driveway with the open knife in one hand. The squealing tires threw rocks in every direction as Tony backed it to the road. I prayed that he wouldn't hit a sharp rock and get a flat. I didn't want him hanging around any longer than needed. Aunt Holly bent down and picked up the tackle box and her fishing pole.

"Let's go fishing, Mac."

"You really are tough, Aunt Holly. I thought Mrs. Grace was afraid of you," I said as I tried to keep up with Aunt Holly's march toward the pond.

She cut me short with cold eyes and a steely face. I didn't say anything else. I followed in silence as we made our way around the pond to the dock. Aunt Holly appeared to walk with a more determined stride than usual, kicking at small rocks on the ground. She dropped the tackle box, and we sat on the wooden dock, our backs to the sun. She began to set up our fishing poles. When she finished, she pushed the fishing pole into my arms.

"You're old enough to bait your own hook," she said.

"Okay," I said meekly.

Aunt Holly sat down on the edge of the dock with her feet dangling over the water. The worm wiggled in my fingers as I carefully threaded him on the hook. Pleased with myself, I cast the line into the water.

"Scoot over here," Aunt Holly said, motioning to the space beside her.

I had a cork bobber and a little sunfish played with the bait but never took it. Aunt Holly fished off the bottom. She didn't look at her line but stared into space, immersed in her own thoughts. It took a good half hour for my heart to stop beating like a drum. The sun felt warm on my back and I placed my fishing pole on the dock and started to pull my shirt off.

"No, don't do that," she said.

Her voice was harsh and cold.

"Okay," I said, and picked up my pole. I stared down at the bobber.

My feelings were hurt. Sometimes I didn't understand the world of grownups just like they didn't understand mine. We sat quietly on the dock, our lines dangling in the water. I bent my head and focused on the lifeless bobber, thinking how my life seemed upside down. I was supposed to be in Kansas City playing baseball and winning a championship. I didn't understand why Aunt Holly was so angry with me. I heard a honk and a lone duck glided out of nowhere and landed quietly on the pond, sending expanding ripples across the glass surface. The lone drake with his green head glistening in the sunlight pushed quietly toward the far bank, oblivious to us. I glanced at Aunt Holly and saw her eyes slowly following the duck until our eyes met. A hand rose and cupped the back of my head, pulling me close until our foreheads touched.

"You know you and that girl are causing me a lot of trouble," she said as she kissed my forehead.

"I don't mean to," I said.

"Don't go looking for trouble because it has a way of finding you," she said.

"I'm not looking for trouble, Aunt Holly."

"I know. You have enough problems and I shouldn't be taking things out on you."

I pulled away and looked Aunt Holly in the eyes.

"Dory's got a mean step-mother."

"Yes she does. I just want you to know that I'm sorry, Mac. That--that woman got me so mad I can't think straight."

"That's okay," I said.

"No. You think I'm mad at you. I'm not really and I shouldn't take it out on you. She's such a hateful old biddy. She made me scared for you."

"I'm going to be okay," I assured her, although deep inside I, too, had my doubts.

"You'd better be," she whispered.

"You okay?" I asked

She took a breath, slowly let it out, and shook her head. Her lips gently brushed against my ear.

"And for your information, I would nail his nuts to the door."

We both started laughing.

14

A warm breeze had started to blow in from the northwest. It picked up the red dust from the driveway and whipped it around like miniature tornados. The last bits of sunlight clung to the horizon, painting the sky with an orange glow and slender rays of light pierced the tops of the trees. Somewhere in the distance a Whip-poor-will sang as the darkness encroached. I sat on a metal folding chair that had once been in the kitchen. Scooter had curled up in his box beside my chair. John and Aunt Holly sat on an old wicker couch. John smoked his pipe, a pouch of Sir Walter Raleigh protruded from his shirt pocket. Aunt Holly balanced a glass of ice tea on her crossed legs with one hand while the other lightly lay on John's leg. Dinner had been chicken wings, boiled potatoes, and green beans. I'd picked the last of the lettuce from the garden and helped by making a salad. The leaf lettuce was tough and Aunt Holly said we should have made a wilted salad. The cream soda bottle in my hand was empty. I closed my eyes and listened to June bugs banging on the window screen. The evening world had come awake.

Aunt Holly had talked to John earlier about Mrs. Grace. He said nothing, only nodded his head. The expressionless face told me he did not like Mrs. Grace's little visit. A glance my way as Aunt Holly told the story told me that John would talk to me later about Mrs. Grace, Dory, and Tony. As was John's custom, you never talked business until after the evening meal. Supper was a time for conversation. You talked about your day, neighbors you saw, and what you had for lunch. Hefty subjects were always kept until later. Sometimes you wished that they'd just spit it out and not wait, but then, some things never change. When Aunt Holly went inside to finish the dinner dishes I knew what would follow.

John stared off into the distance as if something held his interest. He cleared his throat before he began to speak.

"Holly says you all had company today."

"Uh-huh," I replied, trying to sound nonchalant.

"What are you going to do?" he asked.

My hands clasped together, I squirmed on the slick metal and thought of my possibilities. I could say that I wouldn't see Dory but I didn't like that idea. Maybe Aunt Holly could go up and talk to Mrs. Grace about letting me see Dory but that was a stupid idea that wouldn't work. Or I could just pretend Mrs. Grace had never come by and continue to see Dory and die. I really didn't like that idea either. Since I didn't have an answer, I gave the only response I could.

"I don't know."

I emphasized my statement with a deep shrug.

John uncrossed his legs, leaned forward, and rested his elbows on his knees. "What do you think would be the smart thing to do?" he asked.

I threw my head back and sighed.

"Don't see her, I guess."

John clasped his hands together and looked down at the ground.

"Is that what you want to do?"

"No."

"It would be the smart thing to do, though" John said.

"Yeah."

"So what's wrong?" he asked. "You're getting old enough that I can't make these decisions for you. You have to figure it out yourself."

I rose out of my chair and walked to the edge of the porch. "I like her."

"You like her?" John was silent for a second. "Is she pretty?"

I thought about this, mulling over in my mind why I liked Dory. Was she pretty? In my mind I couldn't separate Dory into parts. She came as a whole package.

"I don't know. I just know I like being around her. Something about her is different. I just can't explain it." I turned and looked at John. "I don't understand it myself. I've never felt this way before."

"This seems to be getting out of hand. Your Aunt Holly and I don't want you to get hurt. The Grace family is different than most folks around here. We don't even know what they do. Mrs. Grace does some housecleaning but the story going around is that she has sticky fingers."

"Sticky fingers?"

"Takes things that don't belong to her," John said, tapping his pipe into an old tin can beside his chair.

I crammed my hands in my pocket, and walked to the edge of the porch. Fireflies danced before my eyes in the shadow of the oak trees lining the driveway. In a few more minutes the driveway would be pitch black. I spotted a small, lone figure turning off the road and approaching the house. I pointed for John to see. He pushed out of his chair and stood beside me.

"You have a visitor," I said.

"Neva Murphy. I can tell by the way she walks. She lives just down the road. I wonder what she wants. She usually goes to bed when the sun goes down." John stopped to look at me. "Summer and winter, and she's up before the birds sing." The edges of John's mouth broke into a smile. "She gets more sleep than anyone in Polk County."

Miss Murphy stood about five feet tall. She took long strides that made her head bob up and down as she walked toward us. An old safari hat on her head flopped down over her ears to partially hide her face. A large scarf had been pulled tight over the top of the hat and tied under her chin. She wore a simple white cotton dress that whipped around her ankles and a pair of black Converse tennis shoes that looked like they'd seen better days. A large straw bag hung from one arm and bumped rhythmically against her leg. John stepped off the porch to greet her.

"Hi, Miss Murphy. What brings you out so late?"

Miss Murphy peeked around John and pointed a finger at me.

"Is that your nephew from Kansas City?" she asked. Her high-pitched voice was sharp and irritating.

John turned his head toward me.

"Yes, Mac's staying with us for the summer."

Miss Murphy looked back at John.

"He's the one with the sick dad? Someone told me that when I went into town this afternoon."

"Yes, his father is very sick but we're hoping he'll get better."

John tucked his hand under Miss Murphy's arm and led her to the metal chair on the front porch. John eased her down gingerly onto the chair. He stepped back and sat on the edge of the porch while Miss Murphy dropped her bag beside the chair and carefully untied the scarf. The hat fell off her head into her lap. Short black hair flecked with gray, protruding front teeth, and round, bulging eyes were revealed. Miss

Murphy reminded me of the comedian Imogene Coca who was popular at the time.

"Is something wrong, Miss Murphy?" John asked.

Miss Murphy took a deep breath and sat up straight in the chair with her hands folded in her lap.

"Howard is gone," she said in a whisper.

John stood up and rested his arm against a post at the edge of the porch.

"What happened?" he asked, bending over so he could see her face.

"I don't know. He just flew out the window."

John saw me scratch my head.

"Howard is Miss Murphy's parakeet. She got him three years ago when she visited her sister in St. Louis. I'm sure he'll come back."

Miss Murphy shook her head and stifled a sob.

"I don't think so. He's never been outside. I mean, he was born in a pet shop. Sometimes I let him fly around the house but I'm always very careful."

"What happened?" John asked.

Miss Murphy wiped her nose on her blouse and sniffed.

"I let Howard out of his cage so I could clean it. I forgot that I'd left a window open because it was so hot in the house. There was no screen on the window so Howard flew right to it and away he went without as much as a goodbye."

I edged closer to Miss Murphy. "When did this happen?"

"About two hours ago. I wanted to clean the cage before I started my dinner."

John glanced at me and then placed a reassuring hand on top of her's.

"We'll keep an eye out for Howard. Mac will be out and about. If he sees Howard, we'll try and catch him for you."

John's steady voice placated Miss Murphy for the moment.

"Well... I guess that would be helpful."

John stood up and jammed his hands in his jean pockets. "Don't you worry Miss Murphy, Howard will come back."

"I suppose you're right. Where else can he go?" She stood up and slapped the floppy safari hat back on her head but left the scarf dangling in her hand. "Unless a hawk gets him."

John reached out and touched her shoulder.

"Don't talk like that, Miss Murphy. Think positive."

Miss Murphy nodded her head in agreement.

"You're right." She stepped off the porch and pulled the scarf from her pocket, paused, and slowly turned. "Is Holly making ice cream for the social?"

"You betcha. She'll probably get Mac to help her."

"What social?" I asked.

Miss Murphy strapped the hat on with the scarf as she approached me.

"The school social. We have it every year at the old schoolhouse to raise money for supplies and books. Your Aunt Holly always makes the best chocolate ice cream you ever tasted."

John chuckled. "I think I have to agree with you."

"Most people up north of town go and even some from Bolivar come up," Miss Murphy said, tugging on the scarf.

"Sounds like fun!" I said. "You think me and Aunt Holly will make ice cream tomorrow?"

"I think you better ask your Aunt Holly."

"Well, I better get back," Miss Murphy said.

Suddenly, Miss Murphy's eyes opened wide and she pointed over John's shoulder.

"The school's on fire," she cried.

A bright yellow glow sat on top of the darkened tree line while a billowing black cloud of smoke rose into the air. I stood mesmerized by the flames as the front screen door slammed. John had run into the house. Scooter barked and began to claw at the sides of his box from the sudden excitement. Three minutes later, John ran back out of the house with a bucket, a shovel, and a garden hose slung over one shoulder.

"I called the fire team phone tree. People should be arriving in a couple of minutes! Mac, you stay here with Miss Murphy and your Aunt Holly!" he called back as he disappeared into the dark woods.

Aunt Holly had come out onto the front porch and gathered a wiggling Scooter into her arms, her eyes fixed on the glowing horizon. She pulled Scooter away as he licked at her neck. I moved to stand beside her. The fire grew hotter and the smell of burning wood filled the air,

"What's going to happen now?" I asked.

"The men will try to keep the fire from jumping to the fields or across the road. I'm afraid the school is gone. It makes me sad. I don't know what all the families are going to do," Aunt Holly replied in a whisper.

Miss Murphy's eyes focused on the fire as she inched toward us.

"In just a few minutes our heritage will have gone up in smoke," she murmured.

Aunt Holly grimaced and asked, "Did you go to school there, Miss Murphy?"

Miss Murphy nodded. "As did my husband."

Aunt Holly gave Miss Murphy a quizzical look.

"I didn't know you were married."

"And a son," Miss Murphy added.

"Oh. I just never heard you mention them."

Miss Murphy looked intently at the bright orange glow as it lit the sky.

"It's almost gone," she whispered. "That old building of rotten clapboard was built over seventy years ago."

Aunt Holly and I gazed at the sky as the flames that had leaped and licked at the treetops began to subside and were replaced by a stream of glowing sparks rushing to the heavens.

"John took a hose with him. Is there a water outlet over there?" I asked.

Scooter wiggled and whined, struggling to get out of Aunt Holly's tight grip.

She grimaced and said, "Maybe you should take him."

Scooter willingly fell into my outstretched arms and licked my face as if he hadn't seen me for ages.

"John put an adapter of some sort on the old water pump just in case something like this happened. It won't put out the fire but it might prevent the woods from catching and the fire spreading."

"I lost my son, Phillip, to scarlet fever in the early thirties," Miss Murphy whispered to no one in particular. "Henry died in the Pacific during World War II. Now this is the final nail." She turned to look at us with tears trickling down her cheeks to glisten in the porch light. "My mother said it was part of God's plan. I said bullshit to that."

Without another word, Miss Murphy turned on her heel and walked down the driveway until she faded into the night. In a few more minutes, the sky had returned to black and was ablaze with stars. The only reminder of the fire was the acrid smell of burnt wood and the rumble of voices in the distance. Soon all the cars and trucks that had roared down the gravel road in front of the house had disappeared. Aunt Holly draped an arm around my shoulders and lifted her other arm to see the time.

"How late is it?" I asked.

"Not even nine-thirty," she said.

"Seems later," I said, putting Scooter down on the ground so he could go to the bathroom.

"John!" Aunt Holly cried out and ran toward my uncle as he emerged from the woods with a blackened and grim face.

"I'm dirty," he warned, but that didn't stop Aunt Holly from throwing her arms around him.

"I'm glad your safe," she said, her face nuzzled in the crook of his neck.

"There was no real danger," he said, kissing her on the cheek.

She laughed and slipped her arm around his waist and led him back toward the house. She grabbed my hand as they passed and we all went inside. We sat around the kitchen table drinking ice tea as John recounted what had happened when he reached the old schoolhouse.

"I was the first to get there and it had almost burned to the ground. The wood was so old and dry. It went up it no time. Ben Franklin arrived soon after I did and we hooked the hose up to the pump and started wetting down the grass and trees on the east side of the schoolhouse. Others arrived shortly after that and worked on the other side with buckets, gunnysacks, and shovels. A couple of small fires broke out but we were able to contain them. Once the schoolhouse had burned to the ground, three or four of the fellows had to drive their cars and trucks into the schoolyard and keep their lights on so we could find smoldering areas."

"Did you get them all?" I asked.

John's face looked grim when he responded.

"I certainly hope so. We were lucky we could keep it contained. If there had been a stronger wind tonight, the woods that surround this house would be in flames."

Aunt Holly reached out and caressed his dirt-smudged face.

"How did it start?" she asked.

"We found an old bottle in the woods and it smelled of gasoline. Herb Pitts found it and brought it back for us to see. He gave it to the sheriff but I doubt if we get any fingerprints off of it. Herb's hands were all over the outside."

"So... it was arson? Someone set the fire?" Aunt Holly asked.

"It looks like it."

I shuffled in the chair and thought who would want to burn a schoolhouse down. Of course, I thought of Tony but that didn't make any sense. Tony had left school a long time ago. Now there would be no ice cream social. I suddenly realized that the summer I had planned in Kansas City was now looking pretty dull compared to the first two days in the small country town of Bolivar, Mo.

"That's sad," Aunt Holly muttered to herself.

"A lot of history in that old schoolhouse," John said. He grasped Aunt Holly's hand in his. "Our history."

The room became very quiet. Aunt Holly had been joyous that John didn't get hurt fighting the fire. With the realization that someone had intentionally set fire to the schoolhouse, the mood became very somber.

15

By ten o'clock we'd finished our ice tea. John pushed away from the table and said he was going to call it a night. It was late so Aunt Holly let me brush my teeth at the kitchen sink without bathing if I promised to take a bath in the morning. Scooter tumbled out of my arms into his box, whined for a moment as I undressed, and finally settled down when I turned out the light and jumped into bed. I stretched out in my briefs with the bedroom window open. A black fan hummed on a small table by my bed and blew a steady stream of warm air across my body to fight the humid night. Little beads of sweat lined my forehead. The adrenaline rush I felt wouldn't let go. Folding my hands behind my head, I thought of the last two days: Dory Grace, Tony Grace, Mrs. Grace, Howard the parakeet, and the old schoolhouse burning down. I hadn't thought anything could be more exciting than playing baseball this summer. I mouthed Dory's name and thought of her this afternoon as she'd crouched in the back of Tony's car. She'd held her head in her hands and rocked back and forth. It didn't take a Sherlock Holmes to know that something was very strange in the Grace family. Mrs. Grace had been scary today while Tony seemed like he didn't care. That didn't make sense because Tony had roughed me up because I had been with Dory. Aunt Holly didn't know anything about the Grace family. My thoughts were interrupted by something moving outside my window. I sat up on the edge of the bed and kicked Scooter's box. He gave a small yelp and went back to sleep.

"Hey."

Dory's voice made me jump as I saw her outlined in the window. I searched frantically for something to cover my naked--almost naked--body.

"Don't worry about it," she said. "It ain't no different than this morning."

I heard a faint giggle.

"What do you want?" I asked sharply, swatting at a mosquito nipping at my left shoulder.

She squatted down and draped her hands on the windowsill and sat quietly for a second.

"Tony set that fire to the schoolhouse tonight."

I jumped out of bed and knelt by the window.

"Why?" I asked.

I saw the small shoulders bounce and a faint sob slipped from her lips. I was afraid to say anything. Her head tilted up and the moon painted a yellow halo around her head.

"I asked my step-mother if I could go to school this fall. Tony don't want me to go."

"Why would Tony burn the school down?" I asked.

"Tony never went to no school so he don't want me to go."

"You need to tell the sheriff," I said.

She forced a laugh.

"And make my life worser than it is now?" she asked. "Don't you go telling anybody what I just told you. My life would be misery."

I thought for a second.

"You could stay with Aunt Holly and John."

Dory Grace hung her head. "You don't understand."

"I know Aunt Holly would let you."

"You remember how…" She stopped for a second and stared into the darkness of the woods behind her. My eyes followed hers but I could hear or see nothing. "Remember my secret place," she whispered.

She pushed away from the window and slipped down the side of the house to the front. I sat in the darkness staring out at the empty moonlight yard. An owl hooted in the distance and I slapped at another mosquito nibbling at my cheek. Scooter stirred when I returned to bed and gave a yelp. I reached down and scratched his head and thought about Dory's short visit. My conscience told me that I needed to tell John but I knew I wouldn't. Scooter became more restless. Standing up, he pawed at the small towel that made up his bed. He pawed, turned, pawed again at the towel until it bunched up in a ball. Growling, Scooter pounced on the towel with a vengeance. I laughed and Scooter paused long enough to look up at me for a second before tearing into the towel again in earnest.

All of a sudden, the bed no longer concerned Scooter. Jumping up on the side of the box, he gave sharp, high-pitched yelps at something outside.

"What is it, Scooter?"

I snatched up the wiggling bundle of fur and held him to my chest but he squirmed out of my arms and fell to the floor with a soft thud. Scrambling to his feet he pounced to the window. His legs were too short to reach the windowsill so his front paws clawed at the wall as he bounced up and down, yipping frantically. Rushing to silence him, I knelt down and scooped him up. Holding him tightly in my arms I peered out into the darkness. Tony Grace looked toward the window with a somber face as he walked slowly across the moonlight yard in the direction Dory had gone just minutes before. Scooter barked louder and Aunt Holly came rushing in the door.

"What is going on?" she asked.

She stopped in the middle of the room, her old terrycloth robe swirling around her ankles. With both hands on her hips, her long red hair falling around her face, she peered down at Scooter and me with narrowed eyes. I glanced over my shoulder at the empty moonlight yard and inwardly gave a sigh of relief.

"I think Scooter heard a raccoon or something."

Aunt Holly made an awful face as she stood there for a second as if needing time to process the possibility.

"Well...go back to bed. We have a busy day tomorrow."

Yawning and scratching the top of her head, Aunt Holly turned and trudged back to her bedroom. I stood at the window for a minute longer, searching the shadows for Tony. Scooter nuzzled his head against my armpit and promptly fell asleep.

16

I sat down to a solemn breakfast the next morning. The stench of smoke still clung in the air. Aunt Holly quietly fixed bacon and eggs with toasted homemade bread. She opened a fresh jar of strawberry preserves and sat it on the table with a loud thump. She turned her back to me, picked up her coffee cup, and stared out the window at nothing in particular. John slipped into the kitchen seconds later, nodded his head at me, and sat down.

"Something died last night and it won't come back," Aunt Holly said with a tinge of sadness in her voice.

"I'm afraid so," John replied quietly.

The eggs sat on a large platter with bacon to one side. A slab of fresh butter sat softening on a small bread plate and a large spoon leaned askew in the jar of strawberry preserves. Fresh milk with bits of butterfat clinging to the top of the glass pitcher sat in the middle of the table. John motioned for me to go first. I took my fork and scraped two eggs onto my plate with a healthy portion of bacon.

"Why don't they just build it back?" I asked.

John gave a sardonic laugh. "No money. We hardly had money to keep the stove going last winter. It was the last one-room schoolhouse still operating in Polk County."

"Times change but you like to hold onto some things," Aunt Holly said.

"Why?" I asked. "It wasn't much of a building."

Aunt Holly whipped around with anger in her eyes. I thought she was going to eat me alive. John held out a restraining hand.

"A tradition has passed that everyone in this part of the county wasn't ready to let go of yet," he explained. "I went to that school, as did your Aunt Holly and your mom. That's when your Aunt Holly had pigtails and I'd pull them to get her attention."

"Looks like it worked," I said.

Aunt Holly took a deep breath and gave me a resigned smile. A hand reached out and ruffled my hair.

"I guess there are some things you never want to let go of in life," she said. "I have many fond memories of that school. The friends I've made, many I still have…"

"Sit down and eat your breakfast," John said. "What is done is done. We can't change it."

"You're right, of course, but I don't have to like it."

The rest of breakfast passed in silence except for the scrape of forks against white dinner plates that John bought from a restaurant going out of business. Finished with my bacon and eggs, I lumped a big blob of strawberry preserves on my toast and took a bite. The preserves oozed around and away from my mouth and some fell on my plate.

"The strawberry preserves are great," I said, wiping my sticky mouth with my cloth napkin.

Aunt Holly frowned at the napkin now smeared with bright red.

"Do you love my preserves enough to wash the napkins?" she asked.

"No way," I said, taking another bite of my toast.

"I took today off. You want to go check the cattle?" John interjected.

John took the day off because he didn't want any more trouble from the Grace family. I knew that but I didn't say anything. In fact, I felt safer because he'd be home. I had this faith nothing could hurt me with Uncle John around. Aunt Holly started to clear the table the minute John threw his cloth napkin down on his plate.

"Okay," I said, jumping up from the table. "Can I bring Scooter?"

John laughed.

"I don't know if he can keep up. He's got pretty long legs for a pup so I guess it would be okay."

"I can get a tee-towel and make a sling around your neck to carry him," said Aunt Holly.

"Yeah," I said.

Ten minutes later, John led the way out the back door in a straw hat, khaki pants and shirt, and an old pair of combat boots from World War II. I tailed behind, pushing my old baseball cap around my ears. Scooter hung from my shoulder in a sling, his head resting on his front paws. Dew still clung to the grass at seven-thirty, soaking my converse tennis shoes. I could already feel the heat of the coming day. We walked past the pond and out into the field of little blue stem grass with its shades of blue and green seed stalks waving gently in the soft summer breeze. The grass grew almost to my waist and made a swishing sound against my jeans as we made our way to the fields southwest of the house. We passed the small barn where John kept feed for the one milk cow and stored his Ford tractor.

"You making it?" John asked, looking back over his shoulder.

"Uh-huh," I replied, as Scooter's sling swung back and forth on my neck. "This grass is tall already."

"It is," John agreed. "When we get to the gate, I think we'll leave it open so the cattle can graze here. They'll make short work of it."

I glanced across the road to the neighbor's field, green with alfalfa.

"Why don't you plant grass like the guy across the road?"

John took a careless swipe at the tall grass.

"Tell me how good his grass looks in August. Sometimes the old ways are the best ways. Two years ago when we had a dry summer, his alfalfa died and this grass fed my cattle. It looks like we might have a dry summer this year."

I just nodded because it took everything I had in me to keep up with John's long strides. John stopped at a gate. Chewing on a long grass stem he leaned against it and surveyed the next field. The grass was short and close to the ground. The cattle had eaten the grass down to nubs and the pasture was covered in manure.

"When that manure dries, we'll pick it up and throw it in the manure spreader," he said.

"They just about destroyed this field," I said.

John unlatched the gate and propped a rock against the bottom so it wouldn't close.

"It won't take long for it to come back," he said. He pointed toward the west. "I see the cattle over there."

The cattle were spread out that morning. It took longer than John expected to make his count; two were still missing. We crossed the pasture and John found the next gate open. His mouth formed in a thin line as his eyes searched the field for the remaining cattle. He took off his hat and wiped his forehead with his handkerchief. We'd been out for over an hour and the breeze had turned hot. My throat was dry and Scooter began to squirm in his sling.

"What's wrong?" I asked.

"Someone left this gate open."

"Who did?" I asked, adjusting Scooter and praying that he didn't have to pee.

"I don't know," John muttered, looking at the tracks in the dirt. "Whoever it was, they wore tennis shoes like yours." He pointed at a long footprint near the fencepost where you locked the gate. "Let's see if we can find those cows."

"Do you think they were rustled?" I asked.

John ignored me as we walked across the deserted pasture.

"Soo, cow," John shouted.

The cows had trimmed this field earlier in the spring and young shoots of grass were already pushing up to replace what had been eaten. John told me once that the roots of this prairie grass could grow to a depth of eight feet.

"How many cows do you have now, John?" I asked, carefully stepping around three or four cow paddies.

"With the calves, one-hundred and twenty-four," he answered, picking up the pace as he scoured the field.

I began to pant as I attempted to keep up and steady Scooter's sling at the same time. Scooter was now restless and wanted down. "Do you know which ones are missing?"

"A young cow and her calf. This was her first this spring and he was still on the teat."

The trees lining Mile Branch stood before us. To the south were brush, hills, and trees. I tried to see if I could find Dory's white oak but it was still so far away that it's green top blended in with the others. As I brought my eyes down, I saw crows so thick their number blackened the tree limbs near the creek. A thousand wings flapped and their loud caws sounded like a huge squabble. John was ahead but stopped when he heard the crows. He motioned for me to join him and held his finger to his mouth to make sure I didn't make any noise. He parted the brush and we started toward the loud din of crows. This was what John called the wild area of his farm. There were cactus, wild berries, and briars that pulled at your clothes. The ground had never been cleared because it wouldn't take crops or graze cattle. Sometimes in the spring it flooded but instead of leaving good silt, it usually filled with tin cans, assorted paper, and tree limbs. Aunt Holly said that it was a corner of the farm that God forgot. As we approached the crows, the more fuss they made and some left their perches and started to circle in the air. John stopped and cupped his hands around his mouth and called. Nothing. He cupped his hands and called again, "Soo, Lady. Soo."

I heard the scuffle of feet across the rocky ground as if someone were running away.

"Did you hear that?" I asked.

John's head turned quickly toward the noise and he held his hand up for me to be quiet. We stood there silently for a couple of minutes until we both heard a mournful sound rise out of the thicket in front of us. John started to run. We didn't have to go far to find Lady. She stood on the rocky creek bank of Mile Branch as she attempted to protect the lifeless form at her feet. John stopped and surveyed the gore in front of us. The young calf was dead. Someone had made a feeble attempt to butcher it on the creek bank. They had failed miserably. Bloodied rocks covered the ground and the calf had horrible slices all over it. I looked from John, to the calf, to Lady. John's face became stone cold and white.

A nervous hand brushed across his tightened jaw. "The stupid son of a bitch didn't know what he was doing."

"Was someone trying to rustle your calf?" I asked.

"I don't know what it is. I do know he tried to butcher this calf with a short knife blade. That's why he couldn't get the meat. Let's get back to the house and call the sheriff."

17

Aunt Holly met us at the backdoor with a big smile. It quickly vanished when she saw John's face. He marched past her through the kitchen and into the living room where they kept the phone. Aunt Holly grabbed my arm as I walked by and pulled me back outside.

"What's going on? What's happened?"

"We found a dead calf in the wild area. It looked like we interrupted someone trying to cut the calf into pieces."

"Why would someone want to kill a young calf? Who's calf was it?" she asked.

"Yours," I said.

"No, I know that. I want to know which cow was the mother."

"Oh." I thought for a second. "I think John called her Lady."

Aunt Holly shook her head in disbelief.

"She calved late this spring. I don't think that calf was over two months old. Why would someone attempt to butcher a little calf?"

"There were cuts all over the calf's body where they tried to cut it up. John said she bled to death."

· "It would have been easier just to pick the calf up and take it home. That calf couldn't have been very big."

"I heard someone leave when we started into the wild area. John did, too."

"Did you see them?"

I shook my head. "Nope. They got out of there pretty fast."

John returned outside and let the screen door slam behind him. Aunt Holly touched his arm as he sat down on the back step. He carelessly twirled his cap on his finger.

"Sheriff said a deputy would be right out," he said softly.

"That would be Kelly Duncan," Aunt Holly said.

"Is that Johnny Duncan's kid?" John asked.

"His youngest," she said, turning to go back inside.

John shook his head, twirled his cap again, and stared into space. Scooter had fallen asleep in the sling, so I took him inside to his box. John had gone around to the front porch to wait for the deputy. I had never seen this side of my uncle before and it was both confusing and scary. He displayed a calm face on the outside but I could tell that inside he was ready to explode. So, I just sat there quietly and waited with him. My mind flashed back to the calf lying beside the creek and its mother standing over its body, mourning. I wondered how I would feel if my father didn't make it. Our relationship had just begun to develop. Until recently, he was busy rehabbing our house. He got up at four in the morning and delivered milk all day. Late afternoon he'd come trudging home, nod his head at me, and disappear into the bedroom to change into his other work clothes. Suppertime was usually a time for family conversation but my dad was so tired, he said very little. After supper he'd be right back at it. Last year the house was finished and things had begun to change. I'd look in the bleachers at my afternoon baseball games and there sat my dad in his dairy uniform, watching me. Monthly fishing trips were the norm now instead of just talking about them. A treasure hunt shopping spree in old antique stores had produced a cheap Sears and Roebuck 5-string banjo. We were learning how to play. After so many years, our relationship no longer hid in the shadows. The thought of losing my dad now almost took my breath away.

"Here he comes."

John's hollow voice broke into my thoughts. An old 1937 Ford truck that looked like it had seen better days, turned off the road and roared up the driveway. I guess I imagined an older man with dark black whiskers covering his unshaven face, a dusty cowboy hat pushed back on his head, and a jaw bulging with chewing tobacco. Instead, Kelly Duncan looked to be about twenty-one years old. He wore a baseball cap promoting fertilizer. He popped out of the truck with a big grin on his face, a brand new pair of Levi's, and a long sleeve cotton shirt with a deputy sheriff badge pinned to the pocket. Kelly Duncan gave me a short nod before he bounced toward John with an outstretched hand.

"My daddy says hello. He served under you in the Corp of Engineers in Germany."

John stood up and extended his hand. He wore a thin smile as he took a step to meet Kelly.

"Your dad is a fine man. I was proud to serve with him."

"He says the same about you. Funny how you two met up and all," Kelly replied, slapping John on his right shoulder like they'd been friends for life. Such is the way things are in a small town.

"Yes, it was." John paused for a second. "I guess the sheriff told you what happened?"

Kelly's head rocked and he suddenly became serious.

"Yeah, yeah. It looks similar to another one we had last week. We only found the remains, which amounts to some skin, the head, and scraps. It was a butcher job. The sheriff says it was done with a pocketknife? That don't seem possible."

"By looking at the calf, I'd say the blade couldn't have been over four inches long," John lifted his hands so his palms were facing one another to emphasize the length of the blade. "The meat was hacked off. I think my nephew and I surprised whoever was doing the butchering and scared them off."

"Wow. This other butcher job was done with a similar blade. Still was a chop job. Someone is butchering small calves because they don't know nothing about how to butcher a cow."

"Or they don't have the equipment. I don't think this was someone who rustles cattle. This job was for home consumption."

I don't know why but Tony crossed my mind. Although I had no proof, it had his trademark all over it.

"Tony," I whispered.

"What did you say?" Kelly asked. "Who is Tony?"

"Tony Grace," John said, " a young man who lives at the top of the hill after you cross Mile Branch going toward town. The Grace family moved here recently and they're renting the old Kirkpatrick house. You know, Tom Kirkpatrick was killed in Korea and his wife moved to town to be closer to her folks."

Kelly turned to me. "What makes you think Tony is mixed up in this?"

I shrugged my shoulders. "It sounds like something he'd do."

Kelly turned back to John.

"Well, I can't say he did it but I wouldn't put it past him. I've heard stories about Tony Grace and he sounds like a wild child that was raised by wolves - scary to be around. I caught him wandering along the banks of Mile Branch a couple of weeks back. I asked him what he was doing. He just turned and walked away. A strange kid."

Kelly took off his cap and wiped his forehead with his arm.

"Looks like a good place to start. First we need to see this calf."

Kelly suggested that we take his truck. I grabbed Scooter from his box and hurriedly crammed him in the sling. I hopped in the truck bed and leaned against the back of the cab. The truck started with a jerk and I immediately regretted my decision. The minute Kelly popped the clutch I was tossed forward and rolled over on my side, banging my head against the side of the truck bed. Pushing back up into a sitting position, one hand steadied me against the truck bed while the other wrapped around Scooter so he wouldn't be tossed out of the sling. I decided after this trip that this was my last ride in the bed of a pickup. Finally we arrived where we'd found the calf. The truck came to a stop and John climbed out of the cab and walked back to me. A big grin on his face, he placed his hands on the sides of the truck bed.

"Get a little rough back here?" he asked.

I attempted to scramble to my feet but my stiff legs didn't want to move. Restless and tired of the rough ride, Scooter clawed his way out of the sling before I could stop him. He rolled off my legs onto the truck bed with a thud.

"Come here, Scooter," I yelled.

Scooter had a mind of his own and it told him to get out of there. I rolled and crawled all over that truck trying to catch him. John finally reached down and scooped him up and held the wiggling puppy in his arms.

"Gotcha!"

"Finally!" I said.

John handed Scooter to me and lowered the tailgate. "Why don't you scoot your butt down to get out?"

Sore and tired from the short ride, still nursing my bruises, I bundled Scooter back in my arms and carefully got down to follow John and the Deputy. It seemed extremely quiet except for our footsteps on the rocky ground as we pushed through the brush. The crows and vultures had gone. I knew something had changed from earlier in the day. I glanced at John and saw concern etched in his grim expression. John and Kelly picked up the pace and I scrambled to keep up with them. Scooter had tired of the sling after the ride in the truck. As I stumbled after the two men, images of Monty Hale and every other B cowboy movie star I loved, popped into my mind. Just like my heroes, I had become involved in cattle rustling and I was helping the sheriff bring the bad guys to justice. Oh, what fantasies I had. Boys back then dreamed of accomplishing heroic deeds, saving damsels in distress, of being hailed as a hero. I couldn't know at the time that the changes that summer held in store for me wouldn't involve the typical western scenario, but I'd never be the same. Oh, I wouldn't give up baseball or watching B movies on a Saturday afternoon at the Mary Lou Theater for ten cents. Not right away. Growth comes in sudden spurts and that was my summer to grow. But at that moment the adrenaline pumped through my veins as we neared Mile Branch. I felt an excitement I'd never felt before. A tingling feeling rang through my body that was exhilarating: I felt alive. Caught up in heroic thoughts, I didn't watch where I was walking and I tripped over a half-buried limb and fell to the ground.

"Ow!" I grunted.

Scooter jumped out of my arms as I fell and he ran after the two men. I glanced up to see if anyone saw me fall only to see John and Kelly pass through some bushes and disappear with Scooter at their heels. I felt hurt and betrayed by Scooter. I picked myself up, brushed off my new jeans, and found a new hole in the knee.

You okay?" John asked when I caught up.

Scooter stood at his feet wagging his tail and barking as I approached.

"I'm okay," I said sheepishly.

John turned back to Kelly.

"The calf was right here," Kelly said, pointing at the blood-stained rocks.

John pointed at Lady standing vigil by a barbwire fence, waiting for her calf to come back. "Lady crossed the creek to that fence line since we left. Whoever did the butchering came back."

I never realized that cows could mourn like a human. Her large, brown eyes scanned the woods before her, searching for her calf. Lady turned her head toward us for a second as if asking us for help.

"I tripped back there."

Kelly ignored what I said and continued across Mile Branch until he stood next to the fence line.

"Blood on the ground here. He must have gone this way with it."

John waded through the water, leaving a heart-broken Scooter on the bank barking frantically. I picked him up again and forcibly put him back in the sling.

"Traitor," I whispered and followed John.

Kelly had slipped through the barbed wire fence and stood looking at the ground.

"There's a cow path over here and it looks like it follows the creek toward the road. I see blood."

"Let's see where the blood leads us," John said.

John held the barbed wire fence down while I carefully stepped over. Scooter clawed at my chest so hard that I finally put him back down on the ground. He seemed happy but he couldn't keep up with the two men. Grudgingly, I walked slowly and watched him stop to pee three times, smell every leaf and bush, and then attempt to catch up. I could no longer see John and Kelly but their voices carried in the still morning. I knew we were heading for the bridge and the road that ran on the south side of John's farm. The calf had bled out and there were few traces of blood to follow. Scooter stopped to inspect a small ring neck snake slithering next to the cow path. He barked, fiercely lunged at the small snake, and then just as fast, pulled back a safe distance. In frustration, I scooped Scooter up and ran after John and Kelly.

Mile Branch snaked under a bridge with rusted steel railings that had been built during the nineteen-thirties and could accommodate only one car crossing at a time. I broke out of the woods and stood beside the roadside to see a large open pasture filled with alfalfa on the north side of Mile Branch. Bordered by the road, it spread as far as I could see like a lush green ocean of grass. A tall, tree-covered hill filled with old sycamores and red cedar marked the south side. I crossed the road and looked to my right. Atop that hill sat the Grace house half hidden by the foliage. I imagined Tony Grace hiding in the shadows and watching our every move. John and Kelly stood on the other side of the road close to the creek bank. I read disappointment on their faces.

"I can't tell if a car parked here or not," Kelly said, his hand making a waving motion over an area where the trail stopped.

"Its just hard rock and gravel. The blood trail is gone so I guess we'll never know," John replied.

"You mean that's it?" I said.

"For now," Kelly said.

John 's face was somber as he leaned down and snatched a plume of grass and stuck it in his mouth.

"For now," John echoed.

"What about Tony?" I asked.

"If we can't find a trail to lead us to him, we got nothing," Kelly said with a shrug of his shoulders.

Disappointed, I walked down to the creek bank and commenced to do what any boy does when he sees water: skip rocks across the silent pool under the bridge. A coil of barbed wire that someone had strung across the creek eons ago lay almost hidden next to me. Old and rusted, it blended in with the brownish-red clay bank. I reached down to pick up a particularly smooth and flat rock, perfect for skipping, when I saw the small tuft of black hair attached to one of the barbs. I scanned other barbs and found small patches of hair.

"John! Over here. I think I found something."

"Wait as second, Mac. I'm talking to Kelly," John said impatiently.

My eyes darted across the creek. I saw that a single strand of wire was still strung across the creek. It made a small ripple as the current pushed against it. My eyes followed the wire to a narrow path that led from the creek bank up the hill - up the hill toward the Grace house. Forgetting Kelly and John, I tucked Scooter tightly against my chest and marched across the rocky bank and into the creek. The water was cool as it crawled up my legs. Deeper than it looked, the water rose waist high and my tennis shoes began to slip on the smooth limestone bottom. The water licked at the bottom of Scooter's sling and he began to whine and scratch me to lift him higher. Clutching the sling, I watched minnows dart every which way to escape my intrusion and a school of suckers quickly turned back upstream. As I closed on the opposite bank, I felt an exhilaration I'd never experienced before. I knew what I would find once I reached the bank. I could hear John and Kelly talking faintly in the background. They didn't realize that I had waded toward the opposite bank. The water started to recede and, as my wet body became exposed, I started to shiver, wondering how I could be cold in the heat of the summer. I reached out for a young sapling to pull myself up onto the bank. An old log rocked gently against the bank with a red and white fishing bobber dangling from one of its broken limbs. Old pop bottles, candy wrappers, and old bait tin cans lay scattered around where I pulled myself from the water. I began to search the ground for the barbed wire. Hidden from view because of years of neglect and seasonal flooding, I finally found it joined to a broken fence post laying flat against the ground. The downed fence lay along the path leading up the hill. It didn't take long for me to find another tuft of hair on the barbed wire. My eyes lifted up to see Tony Grace standing at the top of the hill, hands on his hips and watching me with hatred in his eyes.

My heart jumped into my throat as I twirled around and literally leaped in the creek. I knew any second that Tony Grace would follow me and Scooter and I would die. I hit the water belly first and that sent Scooter flying out of the sling and skidding across the water on his back. Suddenly, Scooter started to sink in the water like a rock, only his little head bobbed up and down as he struggled to keep his head above the water. I struggled to my feet and reached for Scooter but I slipped on the slick rock bottom and I fell backward in the water. I sunk under the surface and water poured into my opened mouth. My arms flailed in a worthless effort to regain my balance. I'd always had a fear of the water and this episode only reinforced that fear. The harder I tried to plant my feet back on the slippery limestone, the more I failed. Finally I relaxed, flipped over belly down, and commenced to swim underwater. I reached shallow water and planted my feet on the gravel bottom and stood up, wiping the water from my eyes. I panicked and searched frantically until I heard Scooter's sharp yelp. Scooter sat in John's arms, tail wagging, and happy to see me. John scratched Scooter's head but his attention was directed toward the Grace house on top of the hill.

"Did I see Tony Grace?" he asked.

"I found bits of hide and hair on the barbed wire on the other side," I gasped, attempting to keep from coughing.

"Where?" Kelly asked.

"It's on the barbed wire over there," I said pointing to the fence line leading into the water on our side of the creek.

18

Hurt and disappointed, I walked the rocky road back home in disgust while John and Kelly walked up to the Grace house. After all, I was the one that suggested it was Tony who had killed the calf in the first place. I was the one who found the tufts of hair and hide on the barbed wire. What thanks did I get? John and Kelly firmly sent me home. I was to tell Aunt Holly that John wouldn't be home for lunch. I'd wanted to be with them and take satisfaction as they hauled Tony Grace off to jail. No such luck. John and Kelly didn't even say thank you to me for finding the pieces of fur caught on the barbed wire fence. John grabbed my shoulders, his face inches from mine, and gave me explicit instructions what I was to do: go home and stay home.

The sun beat down on me as Scooter's sling swung gently back and forth. My body was still wet from the spill in the creek and my clothes stuck to me like a second skin. Scooter lay still in the sling for once. The spill in Mile Branch had quieted him for the time being.

I wondered what would happen to Dory if Tony went to jail. Maybe

John and Aunt Holly could take her into their home. Surely the sheriff could see that Dory would be better off away from the Grace family. Sometimes great ideas fall out of the sky for no reason. I stopped and turned to see Kelly and John trudging up the road and it seemed like forever for them to finally disappear out of sight. I quickly doubled back down the road to the bridge and followed the path back to where we found the calf.

I stood on the bank by the wild area and attempted to get my bearings. Dory had taken me to her secret place and showed me an old tablet. If I could look at that tablet, it might have just what the sheriff would need to take Dory out of the Grace home and bring her to John and Aunt Holly. I headed west, following the creek bank until I came to the rocks that formed a dam across the water. Scooter was still as I crossed and only showed his disfavor when I jostled him climbing up on the other side of the creek.

Everything seemed so familiar to me. In my mind, I could see Dory's skinny body leading the way, her bare feet nimbly dodging rocks and the occasional thorn. My eyes scanned the horizon for the giant white oak but from the path it was invisible. I must have walked back and forth on that path for the best part of an hour and found nothing. It made me appreciate Dory's secret even more. Discouraged, I returned home. Aunt Holly didn't notice that I came in the back door from the field instead of the road. She stood at the kitchen counter cutting fresh homemade bread for sandwiches.

"Did John say when he'd be back?" Aunt Holly asked.

"Nope. Just told me to tell you don't fix lunch for him."

"Oh well," she said. "I guess we can put his sandwich in the icebox until he gets back."

When Aunt Holly said icebox that is exactly what she meant. Electricity was still scarce in the county in 1954, so most people had very few electrical appliances. A coal oil stove in the living room heated the house during the winter. Many people still heated with a wood stove. Aunt Holly did have a propane gas stove for cooking. The icebox sat in the far corner of the kitchen next to a washstand. The washstand had a blue speckled ceramic pan and a bar of soap resting on a hand towel. This is where we washed our hands before we ate if Aunt Holly was using the sink and someone else was in the bathroom. The well had a pump house so we did have running water in the bathroom and kitchen.

"May I eat?" I asked.

Aunt Holly's hands rested on her hips as she scrutinized me with a scowl.

"I think you need to go into the bathroom and wash your whole body down before we sit down at the table. I don't want to sit with someone that has fish poop all over them."

Although I grumbled about cleaning up, I stood in the bathtub and held the rubber showerhead that was affixed to the bathtub spigot over my head and let it dribble down my body. The cool water felt good and I thought back on the morning's activities. I tried to picture Tony Grace catching a calf. A two to three-month old calf is not small and with the mother nearby, it was a wonder he caught it at all. I remember when I was six years old, I accompanied John to the field to count the herd and saw a newborn calf. Innocently running toward the calf so I could pet it, the mother charged me. A speedy grab by John kept me from being at the short end of a mother's love. So how did Tony get away with it today?

"Did you get washed down the drain or did you drown?" Aunt Holly yelled.

I quickly picked up the bar of homemade lye soap and finished my shower.

Aunt Holly sat patiently waiting at the kitchen table. A big smile played across her face as I entered with clean clothes and slicked back hair. She reached out and pulled the chair out for me to sit down.

"What's for lunch?" I asked.

"Biscuits left over from breakfast and ham. I bought some potato chips at the store the other day and I opened a jar of dill pickles."

"Sounds good," I said, plopping down in my chair.

"I also have ice tea. I didn't chip the ice until you got back."

"Want me to get the ice?" I asked.

"If you want."

I grabbed two glasses and walked over to the icebox and lifted the lid while Aunt Holly sliced the biscuits and ham. The cool air that washed my face felt good since air conditioning was not a household word back then. An ice pick with worn letters on its wooden handle rested on a small shelf above the icebox. The block of ice, delivered every other day during the summer, had shrunk to half its size since yesterday. I grasped the ice pick in my hand and held the block of ice steady with the other and began to chip away at the edges. I filled the glasses with two or three chunks of ice and returned to the table.

Once we'd settled in, I asked, "Why does God make people like Tony Grace?"

Aunt Holly hesitated before taking a bite of her biscuit.

"I don't know if I can answer that question."

I took a bite of pickle and stared at Aunt Holly as if I could read her thoughts.

"I mean, guys like Tony Grace are scary."

"Uh-huh," she said, carefully picking up a potato chip and delicately nibbling at it until it was gone. "They certainly are. And that, my dear boy, is why you should stay away from the likes of Tony Grace."

"Do you think God makes people like Tony Grace to test us? Mrs.

Brackel, my Sunday school teacher, told me that once. Why would God want to test us by hurting us?"

Aunt Holly laid her biscuit sandwich on her plate and reached across the table to take my hand.

"I don't know, Mac. John and I aren't the most religious types, you know?" She started to say something else, hesitated, and then patted my hand. "I think that's something you should take up with your parents when you get home."

I frowned, not quite understanding. Everyone in my family was religious, or at least I thought so. Aunt Holly picked up her biscuit and took a bite, carefully avoiding my eyes.

"You do believe in God, don't you?"

Aunt Holly pointed at my plate.

"Eat your lunch."

19

Aunt Holly washed a load of clothes after lunch. The washing machine sat on the back porch by two lead tubs. There was only a cold-water spigot and this was where Aunt Holly washed in summer and winter. She used the lead tubs to soak dirty clothes, soak whites with bluing, or to rinse the wash. It would be hard today for most people to recognize that old washing machine. It was a round tub sitting on four legs with an agitator in the middle. A removable lid fit tightly on top to keep in water while washing. Aunt Holly's was electric but some still had a tall handle that you pushed back and forth to move the agitator. On one side sat the ringer that could be extended over the washer. The ringer consisted of two rollers that Aunt Holly would thread the clothes through to squeeze the water out. Then she'd place the clothes in clean water in the lead tubs and soak them. While the wash soaked, she'd fill the washer again and take the clothes out of the tub and back into the washer. She'd agitate a few minutes and then she'd run them through the ringer again, toss them in a basket, and head for the clothesline. During the winter, she hung the clothes in the kitchen. It was a hard chore.

Since I couldn't help with the wash and Scooter had decided to snuggle up in his box, I went out back and threw rocks at an old tin can by the tool shed. I wanted to play with Scooter but I guess he was tuckered out after all that had happened that morning. Finally the sound of rocks pinging off the tool shed got on Aunt Holly's nerves.

"Mac, if you don't stop throwing those rocks against the shed, I'm going to do something crazy. Why don't you go get the poles and go to the pond and fish? I've only got one load left so I'll join you in an hour or so." The screen door slammed shut as Aunt Holly started back to the kitchen. In a flash, the door opened again and Aunt Holly stuck her head out. "And don't fish off the dock!"

I dug worms from the compost pile, grabbed my favorite pole and headed for the pond. It wasn't a huge pond, only about one-hundred-fifty-feet across. A floating dock sat on the south side. In the city a pond this size would have been called a lake. A large willow at the north end made the perfect spot to throw your line in the water, lean back and watch your bobber. Aunt Holly said that's where she went when she needed to think.

I cast the line in the water and the bobber made a ker-plunk sound. A ring of ripples scurried across the quiet surface and dissipated in the distance. Satisfied with the placement of my line, I leaned back against the tree and closed my eyes. I thought about my father; how he was doing and if he was going to get well. I missed my parents, my home, and my friends. As melancholy threatened to overcome me, a wet blop of something hit me on the nose. My eyes flew open and crossed as I stared at the blob of white. I'd been attacked by bird shit. Jumping up, I frantically searched for something to wipe my nose. There was nothing in the tackle box so I used the only thing I had: my shirttail. I ripped my tee shirt over my head and hurriedly wiped my nose clean of the droppings. To make sure I got it all, I dipped my shirt in the pond, wrung out the water, and scrubbed my nose. Satisfied I'd gotten it all, I dropped the tee shirt to the ground.

"I never met a boy who likes to take his clothes off in public like you do."

She stood behind me in a pair of clean and faded overalls and a tee shirt two sizes too big. She had tied her hair in a short ponytail, which made her face seem even thinner and the dark shadows under her eyes more pronounced.

"A bird shit all over my nose," I protested. "What would you do?"

"It ain't a very big bird. I bet it ain't any bigger than a gumdrop."

"How would you know?" I asked testily.

She pointed up at the tree limb above my head.

"That little blue and yellow bird ain't any bigger than a sparrow. Pretty though."

I backed away from the tree and searched in the limbs for the bird. Sure enough, perched directly above where I had leaned against the tree sat Miss Murphy's Howard.

"Howard!"

"Who?"

"Miss Murphy's pet parakeet," I said. "He got out of his cage yesterday and escaped out the window." I waved my arms to imitate a bird flying.

Howard sat on a small limb, his head following Dory as she walked back and forth beneath him. The legs of her baggy overalls made a swishing sound as she admired the little bird.

"He sure is cute," she said. Silent for a second, Dory moved closer to the tree and began to coo. Her thin lips formed a pucker and her tongue made a soft clicking sound. "Come here, Howard. Come to Dory-ory."

"Dory-ory?" I asked.

She smiled and her face flushed. "That's what my daddy use to call me."

"Is that what your family calls you?" I asked.

Her reply was sharp and harsh.

"No! I got no family no more."

My head flew back as if she'd smacked me on the chest. A little smile crept across her face and a sparkle returned to her eyes.

"Maybe you can call me that--in time."

I gulped.

"Okay."

Howard sat on his perch while Dory attempted to coax him to her finger. I watched her in silence. The way she called to the bird was strangely hopeful. She seemed at that moment like a caged bird herself, yearning for the freedom to perch where she wanted. The short sleeve of her tee shirt slid back revealing a light fuzz of hair in her armpit. She looked down at the ground for a second before she took another step closer to the tree. The ugly black mark on the back of her neck jumped out at me. Cooing at Howard, Dory didn't notice me edge up behind her and peer at the bruise, the black and blue forming the imprint of a hand on her creamy skin. My finger reached out and gently brushed aside a tendril of hair to get a better look. Dory immediately spun around and, with both hands planted firmly on my chest, pushed me to the ground. I braced my fall with my arms. Shocked, I gazed up into her anger filled eyes.

"What you doing?" she demanded harshly.

Startled by her outburst, Howard took flight and disappeared toward the house. I pushed myself to my feet and brushed off my jeans. Sullen and feeling defeated, I glanced at Dory standing defiantly in front of me.

"Sorry," I said and walked past her to pick up my tee shirt and slip it over my head.

We didn't say anything for a few minutes. I retrieved my hook, baited it with a worm, adjusted my bobber, and tossed the line in the water. Feeling uneasy, I tried to make myself comfortable on the hard ground even as a cold chill ran through me. I could feel her eyes piercing my back. The rustle of denim drew near and Dory sat down beside me, wrapping her arms around her drawn up knees.

"Why'd you do that?"

"I...I didn't mean anything by it. I saw... the bruises on your neck and I wanted to get a better look." I kept staring into the water, tugging at the pole to jiggle the bobber up and down so the bait would move. "I've done worse. That day at school I jumped on you." Dory buried her face between her knees. "Who did that to you?" I asked. "Tony?"

She raised her head to look at me. Tears had welled up in her eyes.

"You know who did it," she said.

"Why?"

"You don't know Tony."

"What do you mean?"

"Tony's different. He don't take to the ways of most folks." She paused for a second as if conjuring a picture of him in her mind. "I hate him."

"When did he do that?" I asked, nodding to her neck.

Dory leaned back on her arms and stared out at the tranquil water.

"He grabbed me after I talked to you last night."

"I saw him after you left. What did he do?"

Dory ran a hand across the back of her neck.

"It don't matter now. He took off running this morning when he saw the sheriff walk up in front of the house and knock on the door with your Uncle John."

"I know they came to your house," I said. Dory turned and gave me a questioning look. "They found out he tried to butcher one of John's calves."

"He ran like someone had lit a fire to his butt," she giggled and wiped her hand across her runny nose.

"Is Tony your brother?" I asked.

Dory started to answer but her attention was caught as an old car rumbled down the road, leaving a trail of dust in its wake.

"That's someone bringing my step-mom home. I gotta go," she said.

Before I could say anything, Dory raced off, skirting the pond, headed for home. As I saw her hop the fence to the road and disappear out of site, I felt alone. I'd never felt that way around any girl before Dory.

20

I didn't think anything could be more somber than breakfast that morning but supper was more so. I had caught about twenty-four hand-size perch that afternoon and Aunt Holly had told me that if I caught any we'd have them for dinner. I sat in the backyard with Scooter in his box, scaling and gutting fish the rest of the afternoon. John came home in the middle of the afternoon in such a bad mood about Tony that Aunt Holly was consoling him instead of cooking supper. When it came time to eat we had breakfast again.

Scooter had rested from his morning adventure, so I took him in front of the house and watched him terrorize an old knotted rag. He'd take the rag in his mouth and shake his head back and forth with an appropriate growl. Once he tired, he'd drop the rag and start to walk away. I'd grab the rag and shake it over his head and he became rejuvenated and the process would start all over again. Scooter finally tired for good and dropped to the ground like a rock. There was nothing else to do so I killed time by tossing the rag from one hand to the other.

Aunt Holly came out on the front porch and sat down on the old wicker sofa.

"Where's John?" I asked.

Aunt Holly gave a sigh and rested her head against the side of the house and her arms outstretched on the back of the sofa.

"He's in the dining room smoking his pipe and looking over some paperwork. What are you doing?"

"Nothing. Just passing time."

"Scooter looks like he's turned in for the day," she said with a soft laugh.

"Yep," I said.

"Did you give him his flea biscuit?" she asked with arched eyebrows.

I nodded my head. Scooter's belly lay flat against the ground with his legs sprawled to the side. His eyes were closed and he made a soft snorting sound when he breathed. I tossed the rag and it landed in front of his face. He didn't stir.

"Tony hurts Dory," I said, not turning to face Aunt Holly.

"Oh?" she said in that soft voice that invited me to continue.

"I saw it. She got mad at me."

"What did you do to make her mad?"

"I don't know. Then she was nice again. She flip-flops around more than any person I've ever met in my life."

There was a soft chuckle behind me and Aunt Holly coyly said, "And I'm sure you've met a lot of people in your lifetime."

I turned with a sheepish grin on my face and Aunt Holly's arm beckoned me to come sit beside her. I scooted in between her and the arm of the sofa and leaned my head against her soft body. An arm wrapped around me and drew me closer and I melded into her. The sweet smell of lavender mingled with sour perspiration odor.

I didn't mind because I felt safe in her arms.

"Hugs are the best, aren't they," she said.

"Yep."

"Now that we're comfortable, you want to tell me about Dory?"

It took me a minute to start, but once I started, the words came tumbling out of my mouth like turning on the kitchen faucet full blast. Aunt Holly had to slow me down. My nose sniffled, my eyes watered, and sometimes I choked when I talked about Dory. As I look back on this now, I realize that I'd never experienced the type of deranged behavior that the Grace family exhibited toward Dory. There was nothing like it in my friend's families or mine. In my mind, parents were always good to their children. I don't mean that I was completely void of any knowledge of problem families in my neighborhood. I just had never experienced anyone so possessive and physically aggressive as Tony Grace.

"What's she going to do?" I asked when I'd finished.

"I don't know," she answered, one hand lazily pulling a tuff of hair on top of my head. "It certainly is a problem."

"I told her that maybe she could live with you."

There was an awkward silence. My head curled back so my mournful face could look at Aunt Holly. She didn't say anything but I knew she was picking her words carefully because she stopped pulling on my hair.

"Why would you say that?' she asked.

I shrugged.

"I don't know. I think you and John would be good to her."

She gave that soft laugh and started pulling my hair again.

"Thank you. Being a parent is a big responsibility."

"I know," I said. "I think you and John would do just fine.

"You do, do you?"

"Yep. I'm sorry that you and John never can have kids."

There was another awkward silence. A dreamy sad look fell over her and I could tell her thoughts were elsewhere.

"Sometimes things don't happen, no matter how hard you try," she said quietly.

"Still, you'd make a great mom."

She leaned down and kissed my cheek.

"Thank you."

"Makes you wonder why God lets Mrs. Grace have someone like Dory and good people like you and John don't have any kids."

She pulled me tighter and kissed the top of my head.

"Yes, it does make you wonder."

21

I awoke late Thursday morning. I'd slept through the smells of breakfast and the whining of Scooter wanting out of his box. The curtains
flapped from the gentle warm breeze that blew in the open bedroom
window. The humid air was void of the harsh smells I was used to in
Kansas City. Sometimes the putrid smells of the stockyards would per-
meate half the city. Aunt Holly had planted a honeysuckle on the west
side of the house. The first fragrant blooms had opened and drifted in my
window, filling the bedroom with its sweet scent. The only noise was Aunt
Holly in the kitchen and a tractor somewhere in the distance. My eyes
started to close again into a peaceful slumber when I realized that I had
to go to the bathroom. The wooden floor squeaked as I danced around
the room holding myself and trying to find my jeans: they were gone.

"Good morning," Aunt Holly said as I crashed through the doorway
and ran down the hall to the bathroom. "John's in there," she yelled.

I had no other choice but the backyard. I rushed back down the hall,
through the kitchen, and burst outside running straight into the clothes-

line filled with wet clothes. I dashed around the clothesline and made for the side of the tool shed. A sigh of relief slipped from my lips as a steady stream bounced off a rock next to the tree line. After being caught by Dory in my underwear before, I warily searched the woods and waited for her voice to pierce the still morning.

"Did you make it?" Aunt Holly asked when I returned.

"Barely," I said, as the porch screen door slammed behind me. "Where are my jeans?"

"I just put a clean pair on the bed with a clean shirt. Do you want a pair of socks or not."

"I rather just put my tennis shoes on without socks," I said.

There were no wash and wear or permanent press clothes back then. Clothes were ironed. The jeans were still warm, the tee shirt neatly pressed, and I felt a certain comfort when I slipped them on. There is a fresh smell from clothes that had hung on a clothesline over ones dried with softener. Although I reminisce about this, I must admit, I've never heard my mother or Aunt Holly complain about a clothes dryer, permanent press clothes, or softener.

Dressed, I entered the kitchen to see a large wooden bucket with a crank sitting on the table. Aunt Holly stirred something in a large pan on the stove that had the distinct smell of vanilla and cream. Curious, I stuck my head around her body and looked at the creamy mixture.

"Vanilla ice cream," she said. I dipped a finger in the mix and she playfully slapped my hand before I could withdraw it. "Stop that," she said. "Go wash your hands and I'll fix your breakfast."

"Already did," I said, sucking the creamy liquid off my finger. "That's good. What's it for?"

"We've decided to still hold the ice cream social over at the school. Even though the school is gone, that doesn't mean everything has to end."

I made another attempt to snatch a taste of the ice cream but was fended off by a sharp rap of a metal spoon.

"Ouch! That hurt."

"I was ready for you this time," she said, bending over and kissing me on the forehead.

"What's for breakfast?"

"We've already eaten. If you don't get up, you don't get fed."

"No one woke me up!" I protested.

"You're a big boy. You shouldn't need someone to wake you."

"I'm hungry."

"Don't you fix breakfast for yourself at home?" she asked, keeping her attention on the beats of the spoon in the ice cream mix.

I was caught! I did indeed make my own breakfast at home--and lunch. I loved to cook from a very early age and begged my mother to teach me how to fry eggs, bacon, fresh green beans, asparagus, and even broccoli. My favorite meal was chicken fried steak tenderized by using the side of a saucer just like my grandma. I loved to cook at home but being away was different, especially now.

"I didn't hear what you said," Aunt Holly said with a satisfied nod of the head. She took the mixture and set it on a hot pad on the kitchen table and wiped her hands on her apron.

"I can cook my breakfast," I acknowledge with a look of chagrin.

"Good! The skillet for eggs is on the stovetop, bacon and biscuits are on a plate in the oven. You know where to find the eggs."

I picked up the skillet and started to turn on the burner when I remembered something. "Didn't you just say you were going to cook my breakfast?"

She turned to me, the large spoon she held covered with vanilla ice cream mix. "I lied," she said and took a big lick at the spoon. A spot of mix rested on the end of her nose.

We both laughed.

After breakfast I placed my dishes in the sink and sat back down at the table.

"I forgot to tell you. I saw Howard yesterday."

Aunt Holly whipped around with a wet washrag in her hand and a blob of soapsuds fell on the kitchen floor.

"Where?"

"He was sitting in that willow tree down by the pond. He shit on my nose."

Aunt Holly laughed.

"He did not!"

"Yes, he did. Dory came by just as he got me on the nose."

"What happened to Howard?" she asked.

"I don't know. He got scared and flew off."

Aunt Holly finished what she was doing and took off her apron and threw it on the kitchen counter before joining me at the table.

"You've got to tell Miss Murphy that you saw him. She'll be thrilled. She'll be over later."

"I will. I had hoped to catch him but he was too high."

Aunt Holly chuckled as her finger traced the ridge of my nose. "And don't use the word shit."

"I won't."

I didn't tell Aunt Holly that Dory and I fought and that is what scared poor Howard away.

"Tom Maas is going to bring extra ice for us today so we can make ice cream."

"Where are you going to keep it?" I asked.

"John has a cattle trough in the smokehouse and we're going to fill that with ice. With a canvas tarp over it, it should last until tomorrow night."

"Are you just making vanilla?"

"Tomorrow--chocolate."

"Good," I said and rubbed my stomach.

Aunt Holly leaned forward and rested her elbows on the table, cradling her head in her hands. A thin smile on her face, she gave me a goofy look.

"You really like Dory, don't you?"

"I guess."

"Do you like her as a friend or a girlfriend?"

"I don't know. I've never had a girlfriend before. I like her. I like her a lot."

I tried to picture Dory as a boy to see if I would like her just as much but that didn't work. I sure didn't like Dory because of the way she looked. Half the time I was around her, she had a distinct odor and her hair was stringy and oily. I wondered what drew me to Dory, this girl with the baggy clothes, the skinny body and pale face. For some reason, Dory was what I wasn't and that made me want to be around her. I was shy, hesitant, and lacked a lot of self-confidence. Dory, on the other hand, was just the opposite. Beaten by her brother and hidden by her stepmother, Dory's spirit didn't seem to falter. I remembered when I first met her by the school she told me she wanted to die but the very next moment she was rolling on the ground with me and laughing. Dory Grace bounced back again and again. No matter what happened, she survived. I wanted that. I needed a lesson in survival. My father was hospitalized with a stroke and recovery was slow in those days. I hid my fragility, or thought I did, and I tried not to think about my father in Kansas City. I told myself I was on vacation for the summer. Dory helped me face my world.

"Does she like you?"

I felt Aunt Holly's penetrating eyes.

"I don't know," I said slowly. "Maybe."

"Well, she sure comes around a lot for someone that doesn't. No one can seem to keep you two apart."

I thought for a second before I replied.

"Dory… is just different. I can't explain it to you."

Aunt Holly reached out and clasped my hand in hers.

"You don't have to."

We sat there for a few minutes while I mulled this over in my mind. That is one of the reasons I liked to talk to Aunt Holly. She never pushed, just listened, and asked a lot of questions. Her soft hand rubbed mine and I found it very comforting.

The phone rang to interrupt my thoughts.

"I'll get it," Aunt Holly yelled.

John came rushing into the kitchen and waited to see who was on the phone. Aunt Holly placed her hand over the mouthpiece.

"Tom is delivering more ice than usual because of the ice cream social. Do we want three blocks of ice or four?" she asked.

"Make it four," John said, not hiding his disappointment. I'm sure he was hoping it was Kelly with word they'd caught Tony. He slid a kitchen chair out and sat down beside me. "Holly says we're going to have fish tonight. Did you hear that?"

"No," I said.

I looked at Aunt Holly but she had her back to me.

"Do you think I need to check those fish to see if they're scaled and cleaned properly?" John asked.

"I don't think that will be necessary," I answered with a smug look, folding my arms across my chest.

John turned the crank on the ice cream maker and frowned.

"I think this needs some oil. We're going to wear Mac out with that stiff crank. I'll get the oil can."

I turned to Aunt Holly as John started to ransack an old metal cabinet on the back porch for his oil can.

"I get to help?

"You get to turn the crank."

After John oiled the crank and Tom Maas delivered the ice, we got down to the serious business of making ice cream. The ice cream maker was placed in a big washtub in the middle of the kitchen floor. I turned the crank while Aunt Holly chipped ice and layered it around the turning container followed by a layer of salt. The icy cold water rose higher and drained out a hole near the top of the wooden bucket into the washtub. Every few minutes, Aunt Holly would tell me to stop and she'd check the ice cream. We were finished by mid-morning. The remaining ice had been placed in the water trough with the canvas over it. Miss Murphy came by with some fresh strawberry ice cream she'd made and sat it on the kitchen table. John immediately rose from a kitchen chair and took it to the tool shed. Miss Murphy wore a man's khaki shirt, faded and worn blue denim overalls that appeared two sizes to big, and a large floppy straw hat tied under her chin by a faded red ribbon.

Aunt Holly poured a cup of coffee for Miss Murphy and sat it down in front of her.

"I was going to call you this morning, Neva."

"Oh? What did you need?" Miss Murphy asked, blowing on the hot coffee.

"Well, I think I have some good... well, let's just say news about Howard."

Miss Murphy hands were shaking. She grasped the coffee cup with both hands and sat it down on the table.

"What news?" she asked, the slack cheeks jiggled as she waited.

Aunt Holly suppressed a smile. She leaned forward as if sharing a grave secret with Miss Murphy.

"Mac saw Howard yesterday afternoon down by our pond."

Miss Murphy gazed at me with saucer-sized eyes. Her mouth formed a perfect "O" and her hand shook as she reached out to grab my arm.

"Where did you see my Howard?" she asked with a tremor in her voice.

"Like Aunt Holly said, down by the pond. He pooped on my nose."

Her eyes crinkled closed and her hand rose and covered her mouth to hide the light cackle.

"I do declare, that sounds like my Howard. Now that you told me that, I'm going to keep my eyes open for him." Playfully she dug a hand in her shirt pocket and pulled out a handful of birdseed. "I'm ready for him if I see him." She carefully poured the birdseed back in her pocket and sat back in the chair with a triumphant smile on her face. "How did he look?"

"He looked fine," I said.

"I knew he would."

22

Finished with the ice cream, I left Aunt Holly in the kitchen and ambled out to the front porch. I crammed my hands in my pockets and glanced up to see dark popcorn shaped clouds slowly move across the sky. The weatherman had said earlier on the radio that they wouldn't bring any rain. The drought and warm temperatures would continue. The temperature would be in the middle nineties to upper nineties, which was hot for this time of year. Everything was calm. John had taken the day off again. He had taken the truck and gone in to see about selling some of his hay later in the summer. Many of the surrounding farmers who had planted alfalfa would have to buy hay by the end of July if the drought continued. Miss Murphy had returned home with the renewed hope that Howard would come back to her. Aunt Holly and I didn't want lunch since we had snacked all morning on ice cream mix until we almost made ourselves sick. After she finished washing up our mess in the kitchen, Aunt Holly planned to take a short nap. With the house quiet my thoughts turned to Dory.

John had mentioned before he left for town that there had been no word about Tony Grace. The sheriff had questioned Mrs. Grace yesterday and planned to pay her a surprise visit today. I hoped in my heart that Tony had decided to run but I knew he wouldn't. As long as Dory was in the Grace house, Tony wouldn't be far away. The attraction that Tony had for Dory was an obsession that defied reality. In Tony's mind, Dory belonged to him. She was a possession to do with what he wanted. Just the thought of his obsession sent shivers through me. I didn't think that I could have been as strong as Dory. Maybe that is what drew me to her, that uncompromising strength to never give up. I made a mental note to tell Dory she should entrust her notebook to Aunt Holly so Tony couldn't ever get his hands on it.

"Mac? I'm going to take that nap now and there's a little dog asleep in his box." Aunt Holly stood at the screen door, holding it ajar.

"Okay. I think I'll take a walk."

I got up and started to hop off the front porch when her firm tone stopped me.

"Whoa there. I need to know where you're going."

Aunt Holly gave me that look that said no sneaking around.

"I don't know. Probably go over to the old schoolhouse and look around. Then I might go down to the creek for a while. I won't go far--I promise."

"I want you back by three-o'clock. No if, ands, or buts."

"I don't have a watch," I protested.

Her hand reached into the pocket of the men's jeans she was fond of wearing and produced an old pocket watch.

"John bought this a couple of years ago. I've wound it and set the time. You just remember to use it. Okay?"

"Okay, I promise," I said.

"Be careful," she said as the screen door closed.

The path to the old schoolhouse had been well worn through the years. The stench of burnt wood became stronger the closer I neared the clearing. The path opened up and I could see the clearing and burned rubble. I wondered how long it would take for the smell to dissipate. The old stone stoop stood defiantly intact among the rubble where the front door of the schoolhouse once was. I remembered Dory throwing me a message when I stood in the backyard in my underwear. She was sitting on that stoop when I'd gone to meet her.

I don't know what brought me back to the school. There certainly wasn't any attachment or sentimentality that brought me. Something just drew me that I couldn't explain. I walked around the burnt embers, kicking at pieces of blackened wood with strange looking square nails. The cast iron frames of the student's desks stood in perfect formation in the middle of what had been the schoolroom, their wooden desktops gone. Aunt Holly had cried over the school fire and I now understood. A piece of history, her history, had died the other night.

I sat down on the stoop where Dory had sat earlier. I glanced around at the thick growth of thin red oaks struggling to reach the sun. Bushy underbrush stood at the edge of the trees forming a green ring. The brush opened up near the southwest corner of the clearing. I assumed that was where the cow path continued. That's when I saw the yellow ribbon tied to a bush. I didn't remember seeing the ribbon before. As I approached the bushy undergrowth, I realized that was where my journey began to Dory's secret place. My fingers reached out and fumbled with the ribbon. I pulled it lose, threaded it around my fingers, and stretched the ribbon tight between my hands. The word secret printed in large, black letters jumped out at me. Dory needed me.

I started off at a trot, south through the brush. I knew she was hiding from Tony. I followed the tree line of the south pasture, my eyes continually searching for any sign that Tony was following me. I now understood how Dory felt that first day she took me to her secret place. Her eyes had searched the woods. She'd listened for the slightest sound that was different. Tony could slide in and out of your life in a matter of seconds. A chill ran through my body because Tony always seemed to appear out of nowhere when you least expected him. I wondered what he would do if he caught me out alone. I remembered the butchered calf in the wild area. I thought I would be relieved when I finally reached the woods and the creek but my fear seemed to grow. I felt naked while walking the open field but the woods made me feel vulnerable. Following the tree line I cautiously reached the place where I could cross the creek. Taking a deep breath, I glanced over my shoulder before I slipped through the brush toward the creek.

It was quiet. Sunbeams splintered through the trees and a perfect picture of the opposite bank was reflected in the languid pool of water. I found the rocks where Dory and I had crossed the creek. With my arms spread wide like a trapeze artist, I stepped out on the rocks. As the water flowed over my tennis shoes, I was glad I'd left Scooter behind. Reaching the other side, I jumped up on the opposite bank and almost slipped back into the water. My hands grabbed a small sapling. I regained my footing and started to stand up when I slipped again and fell flat on the ground. That's when the rock sailed over my head and hit the tree behind me, only to bounce off and land two inches from my nose. I flattened my body hard against the ground. I didn't hear anything but the pounding of my heart in my head and the quick intake of my breath.

Tony had followed me.

I feared that this might be my last day on this earth. I'd never see my parents, Aunt Holly and Uncle John, or Dory ever again. It would be foolish to think that I was a match for Tony. He was stronger, faster, older, and he always had the look of death on his face. I listened. All was silent except for water running over the rocks in the creek. I thought of the wild rabbit I saw in my backyard last winter. It sat frozen in time, afraid to make a move lest I see him. Fascinated, I'd stood completely still and waited for him to move. Finally, taking one step off the porch, I spooked the rabbit and he ran and dodged until he found refuge in some small brush that grew along our fence line.

Now, I was the rabbit.

Should I wait and run at the last minute? I remember the rabbit's ears standing straight up as if he were listening to every sound. I wanted to have big ears like that rabbit. I closed my eyes and focused on the sounds around me. I heard the creek, birds dithering in the branches of a nearby tree, the distant drone of an airplane somewhere overhead but other than that, nothing. Like that rabbit, I couldn't wait until the last minute when Tony rushed me. Then it would be too late. I had to act.

Rising slowly to my feet, I waited for the next rock to sail through the air and hit me. An immense sense of relief flooded me when nothing happened. My eyes cut to the right where the rock had come from and I saw nothing but trees and brush. I drew a deep breath and gritted my teeth. I carefully started on my way again.

I passed the tree line and emerged into a pasture. I looked up the tree-covered hill ahead of me. I could barely make out the towering white oak with its majestic spread of branches like a kindly old man's beckoning arms. I wondered why I didn't find Dory's secret place yesterday but now that I knew where I was going, it would be easier than yesterday.

The second rock flew past me and hit a small sapling to my left. I started to fall to the ground when the realization came to me: Tony needed me. The rocks were his way of prodding me to move faster. He wanted to find Dory's secret place and I was the means to help him find it. The thought of leading him to Dory was terrifying. I couldn't trust what Tony would do to her or to me. Somehow I had to lead him away from the secret place, away from Dory. At the same time, I had to save myself.

I turned and searched the path I'd taken. Since I knew that Tony would be hidden from view, I again started up the cow path, only faster because that is what Tony would expect me to do. I had to think. Somehow, I had to lose Tony and warn Dory. But how? Fate played into my hands that day. I hadn't walked ten yards when another cow path I'd failed to notice earlier led to my left and appeared to circle the hillside. I took this path. If Tony found out that I had tricked him, any hope that I might have had of staying alive was now gone.

The path was rougher and less traveled. My feet slipped on loose rock and sent me face forward on the ground. I picked myself up and stumbled on. Sometimes I would hide behind a tree and wait to see if Tony showed himself. When nothing happened, I started again. The trees were becoming thicker and closer together. It would have been difficult to break from the path and disappear into the brush. Traipsing through the trees that surrounded me would be like a steel ball in a pinball machine. I could never go in a straight line, only bouncing back and forth off the trees.

Ten minutes later I came to another fork in the path. One led down the hill to my left and the other continued straight ahead. I hesitated, not knowing which path to take. An idea popped into my head that might let me lose Tony--at least long enough so I could warn Dory. I reached into my back pocket and pulled out a white handkerchief that Aunt Holly had placed in there earlier. Aunt Holly is a creature of habit and every man needed a clean white handkerchief in his back pocket.

"It is not just to wipe your nose. You never know when you're going to need a rag or something when you are working out in the pasture. You can tie it around your head for a sweatband or soak it in the creek to help cool you off. A handkerchief is a must in the country."

And it might just save my life--and Dory's.

I unfolded the handkerchief and rolled it up in a ball so it wouldn't look neatly ironed. Walking straight ahead for about ten feet, I dropped the handkerchief beside the path, hoping that it didn't look too obvious. Now I had to hide. I stepped off the path into the trees and worked my way downhill until I found three small cedar trees about three feet high and growing close together. I quickly dropped down out of sight behind the trees and waited. It seemed like forever before Tony finally appeared. In my mind I'd pictured Tony stealthily following me, like an Indian scout. Instead, he walked along as if he didn't have a care in the world. The slingshot was clutched in his right hand and a cotton bag hung around his neck, held by a piece of rope. I didn't know for sure but assumed that he carried rocks for the slingshot in the bag. His step slowed cautiously as he approached the fork in the path. He started to follow the path to his right but then he stopped to consider the path that meandered back down the hill. If he took that path my hiding place would be exposed. I think that was the first time I ever saw panic on Tony's face. He was cunning like a fox but he had no deductive skills and it showed in the confusion on his face. He was only twenty feet from where I hid and I feared he could hear me breathing. I gulped when Tony started down the hill toward me. His eyes took one last look back and that's when he saw my handkerchief.

He giggled like a child.

"Got ya," he whispered.

I waited long after Tony was out of sight before venturing from behind the cedar trees. Quietly extracting myself from the woods, I hurried back the way I'd come and hopefully to Dory's secret hiding place.

23

The tall grass brushed against my legs as I hurried to warn Dory. My eyes canvassed the hillside expecting any minute to have Tony leap in front of me. Even though I'd tricked him, I knew it wouldn't take long for him to realize it and double back. I hoped he'd take the other path that led back down the hillside. My body jerked at the realization that if I met Tony out here alone and after what I'd just done, I was dead. Tony had no fear. He could easily overpower me and no one would know the difference. My mouth was dry and I quickened my pace. Every time I heard a snap or pop I jumped, fearing that it was Tony. I saw a dozen places that he could easily hide my body.

Suddenly the landscape didn't feel familiar. My mind had been focused on Tony instead of where I was going. There were more cedar trees and the path started angling back toward the creek. The sound of water played in my ears and I realized I'd missed the path. I started to turn around when a voice came out of nowhere.

"Hey."

I yelped and jumped back. My heart pounded like it was preparing to leap out of my chest. My one free hand reached up and clasped my throat as a skinny old man with a white fuzzy beard stepped from behind a tree. He wore faded bib overalls and no shirt. His hands were crammed into his front pockets and a shotgun hung loosely in the crook of his arm, the muzzle pointed toward the ground. A dirty felt fedora was pushed back on his head. A thin smile swept across his unshaven face exposing yellowed teeth. I leapt back, frantically searching for an escape route.

"You John's nephew, ain't you?" he said.

I took another step back.

"Uh-huh."

"You look kinda like John. Got his nose."

I unconsciously reached for my nose.

"I'm Everett, Everett Jackson. I live on the hill back here. You can barely see my house from the road."

I hesitated before answering, "I'm glad to meet you, Mr. Jackson."

"John's a good man. Gave me almost quarter side of beef last year when me and the wife were having a hard time. I raise goats and make cheese and had a bunch with mastitis. Didn't have money for a vet. John helped me tie 'em down to give 'em the right shot. He's a good man."

I nodded my head like I knew what he was talking about. "I gotta go, Mr. Jackson. I'm looking--I mean--I need to go back."

Everett Jackson stepped forward and nodded. "She's up there. That's why I'm here, to make sure her brother don't find her."

I gulped. "You know her secret place?"

"My property. Sometimes she comes over to the place and helps my wife--when she can. Hard for her to get out of her brother's sight. I replace limbs on her roof when the leaves die."

I took another look at Everett Jackson and realized that once you saw past his ragged appearance he was a very simple, caring man.

"Does he know where it is?" I asked.

"Naw. I try to keep my eyes peeled so I can scare him off. He doesn't come this way often because he knows about Oscar." He proudly unbent his arm and the shotgun dropped and fell into his hand. "Oscar has a way of deterring Mr. Tony."

I laughed in relief.

"You are her friend," I said.

"Of course. Now if you want to see her, go back the way you came and when you get to a big rock on your right with two cedar trees behind it, turn off the path and go straight up. You'll find her."

"Thanks," I said over my shoulder as I started back up the path.

"Tell her I said hello," he called after me.

I turned back to wave but he had already disappeared from view.

I found the rock and brushed between the two cedars and started straight up the side of the hill. I felt a sense of relief when I spotted the tall white oak reaching for the sky. A goat bleated off to my right and I wondered how close Everett Jackson's house was to Dory's secret place. The terrain was rough and my tennis shoes kept slipping on loose rock. I didn't remember it being this difficult when I'd followed Dory the first time. Finally I stood in front of the small lean-to: it was empty.

"Dory?" I said quietly, afraid that I might be overheard.

Her voice came back in a whisper.

"What do you want?"

"I want to talk," I said.

"You sure you weren't followed?" she asked.

"No, I wasn't followed."

I expected Dory to emerge from behind the large trunk of the white oak but she stood up beside a bush to my right. Cautiously searching the hillside, she motioned toward the lean-to. I followed and we sat down on the ground cross-legged.

"You hiding from Tony?" I asked.

She nodded.

"Sheriff thought he'd be in the next county by now," I said. "Your mom said he'd left and she hasn't seen him."

Turning coldly furious eyes to me Dory growled, "She ain't my mom! She'd lie to her own momma."

We sat there in silence. I looked out over the valley below wondering where Tony was at that moment. Avoiding her angry eyes I surveyed the lean-to. Nothing much has changed.

"I got a jug of water by the tree-- want some," she said.

I licked my dry lips. "That would be good."

She hopped up and disappeared behind the lean-to. In a second she was back carrying a glass jug full of water with a cork stopper seated in the top.

"Here, I just filled it up this morning."

The warm water slid down my parched, aching throat and dribbled at the corners of my mouth. The bottle belched and a slug of water splashed down the front of my shirt.

"God, I gotta teach you how to drink, city boy!"

She laughed and put her finger on my wet chest. The minute I looked down at her hand she flipped her finger up and caught my nose, which made her laugh even harder. I felt like a fool but I said nothing. Dory quit teasing me and picked at a sprig of grass.

I wiped my mouth with the back of my hand. "You can't stay here," I said.

"Why not? Everett's wife, Theodora, brings me cheese and bread to eat. I have water and I can take a bath in Mile Branch."

I picked up a small stick and pushed it through the eyelets on my tennis shoe.

"Did you say Tony came back?"

She laughed.

"He ain't never went away." Her voice became soft and distant. "He'll forever be a part of my life."

I tossed the stick down and placed my hand on her shoulder. She stiffened and looked at me with those large, brooding eyes.

"I know. He followed me for a while today."

Dory pushed to her feet and placed both hands on her head.

"My God, he'll find me for sure."

"I lost him," I said. I told her about what had happened earlier on the path.

"Ha! No one loses Tony. He's like a dog on a rabbit."

"I want you to come live with my Uncle John and Aunt Holly. They'll take care of you." Dory gave a snort and turned away. She continued to pick at the grass. "Why don't you believe me?" I asked.

She didn't say anything for a moment and I actually thought she was thinking about it.

"I like it here," she said.

"He'll find you," I shouted.

A sad, defeated look swept across her face.

"He always does," she whispered. A small tear crept out of the corner of her eye. She looked away so I couldn't see it.

"Look, they're good people and they're fun. I know you'd like Aunt Holly."

I don't know how long I pleaded with Dory to return with me to my aunt and uncle. The words seemed to fall on deaf ears. Exasperated and tired, I finally gave up and just sat with her. I could no longer conjure up the right words to convince her that coming back with me was the safest thing she could do. Suddenly, we heard footsteps behind us. Dory shrieked as Everett Jackson came tumbling around from behind the lean-to. His face told it all.

"You better get out of here. I just saw Tony and he's heading this way. I'll delay him but I know he's looking for both of you."

"Come back to my house," I said.

Everett's head bobbed in agreement.

"If he catches Mac, it will be bad."

Dory scrambled to her feet.

"You go back home. I can take care of myself."

Everett took a step forward and rested a hand on her shoulder.

"We can't trust what Tony will do. He ain't like everyone else and he's mad right now. He's mad at you."

Dory thought for a second and then nodded her head.

"I'll go."

"Don't go back the way you came. Follow the cow path west for another one hundred feet and you'll come to the rock foundation of an old house long gone. Turn north. You'll come to Mile Branch almost as soon as you turn and you'll have to wade across but it ain't deep. You won't have a cow path but you can follow along the edge of the pasture until you get to the woods."

24

Dory didn't say anything. With a simple nod to Everett she turned and started walking west. I don't think she even looked back to see if I was following. Her bare feet slapped down on the hard ground like she had boots on while I scrambled to keep up. I didn't say anything. I saw a new determination in her that I hadn't seen before. We didn't walk far before we found the house foundation, which was just as Everett had described. The foundation was nothing more than a rectangle no bigger than a small bedroom and the rocks rested on top of each other without the benefit of mortar to hold them together. I marveled at how they could have supported anything, much less a small house. Dory immediately turned north.

Dory didn't stop when we reached Mile Branch. She grabbed a small sapling by the bank and slide down into the water and started across the small pool like an experienced hiker. My attempt sent me skidding down the bank and I landed in the creek headfirst. Spitting water out of my mouth, I found my balance and followed Dory. She'd reached the opposite side and hadn't even looked back to see me fall in the water. By the time I reached the other side of the creek, she was already waiting for me at the edge of the tree line and looking out at an expansive field of golden grass.

I caught up with her and asked, "What is that?"

"Wheat. I've never seen any around here before. Some folks grow it up in Hickory county on the Wheatland prairie but I don't know if it ever did well."

I'd never seen wheat before although I live next door to Kansas, a large wheat growing state.

"It's pretty," I said.

Dory shrugged and turned to face me.

"Why'd you come to my secret place?" she asked with a grim look on her face.

"I found the ribbon," I said, reaching into my pocket and holding it up for her to see.

"Oh," she said. "I forgot I left that. I really didn't think you'd find it."

"I wanted to see if you were okay."

"And Tony followed you."

I shoved my hands in my pockets.

"I was real careful."

"Careful or not, he's near."

I asked, "How do you know?"

She turned her gaze to the wheat field edged by a large stand of trees on the east and north.

"I feel him."

"How can you do that? Anyway, Everett said he'd slow him up."

Dory laughed.

"Everett ain't going to slow him up. Don't you understand, Tony ain't never going to leave me alone." Her face became rigid, her lips firm. "I ain't going back. I'll die before I go back."

Without another word, Dory emerged from the shelter of the trees and plunged into the wheat field, blazing a path northward. My wet jeans clung to my wet skin and I felt like someone had wrapped me in a hot towel. I thought that Mile Branch had taken a liking to me since I ended up in the water all the time. I glanced at Dory. The wet bottom of her drab, gray dress clung to her buttocks as she walked but she didn't seem to care or notice. Her arms swung in a wide arc as her thin body cut its way through the wheat.

"We should be to the road that runs by your uncle's place in a bit," she said.

"How long?" I asked.

"Ten--maybe fifteen minutes."

"That long?" I asked.

"We're heading northwest, not north. This wheat field ends pretty soon and we'll have to walk a short ways through some trees."

Her voice was light as if she didn't have a care in the world but her eyes kept scanning the tree line to our right and straight ahead.

"Aunt Holly will fix us something to eat when we get there."

"Good, I could do with something."

"Me, too."

"Your folks religious?" she asked over her shoulder.

"Huh?"

"I asked if they're religious?"

"Not particularly but they're good people," I answered.

"Good."

"I don't understand why you asked me that," I said.

"God don't seem to live on my side of the road," she said simply.

I had no reply to that. Dory stopped, her eyes searching the tree line and the surrounding fields.

"What's wrong?" I whispered.

One finger went to her lips, the other arm flapping at me to be quiet.

"Shh. I heard something."

"What was it?"

"Tony," she mouthed.

"You sure?" I asked with a slight quiver in my voice.

She nodded her head slowly and motioned for me to follow her. This time she started to run and again I was glad that I hadn't brought Scooter with me. Her dress billowed and floated in the air as she ran while my jeans seemed to cling to my legs and slow me down. Dory's long, thin legs slid through the wheat with ease and in less than a minute she was starting to outdistance me. I was used to running short distances in a baseball game, not long distance running. Dory stopped and waited for me. I reached her and my shoulders drooped as I gasped for breath. Dory grabbed my hand and without another word started running, pulling me along behind her.

The trees to our right curved around and now stood between the road and us. By the time we reached the trees, Dory was tugging me. I dropped to the ground and gasped for air. Dory dropped beside me, panting.

"I guess city boys can't run," she said.

"I'm sorry." I turned around and looked at the trees behind us. "Do we have to go through that mess of trees before we get to the road?"

"Yep, unless you want to walk another quarter-mile around 'em."

"You've been here before?" I asked.

"Once--with Tony. He was looking for a cow to butcher."

"How far to the road?"

Dory closed her eyes and gritted her teeth.

"Little bit further than it is from your place to the old schoolhouse."

"That isn't far. Let's go."

I started to jump up but she pulled me back down.

"Wait. I been thinking. Maybe we should cross the road and then double back around to your place."

"Miss Murphy lives down this way. We might be able to stop in her place and ask for help. She could call Aunt Holly."

"Might work," she said.

For the first time since I'd left I looked at my watch: three-thirty. I was late. I jumped up.

"We have to go. I was supposed to be back home half an hour ago!"

"Maybe your aunt is looking for you," she said, a hint of hope in her voice.

"I hope she's still taking a nap," I said.

There were no cow paths or walking trails to follow in this patch of woods. I led the way this time. It was like a maze. The trees grew so close together they blotted out the sun. Intermingled with the red oak were large trees with black trunks and crooked limbs. Impossible to walk in a straight line, we meandered around the thin tree trunks hoping we kept to the right direction. The ground was covered in acorn shells and Dory's bare feet made the going slower.

"Ouch!"

I turned at her cry to find her balancing with her left foot in her hands.

"You okay?" I asked.

"Thorn in my foot," she moaned.

"A thorn?"

Dory yanked a long viscous thorn from the bottom of her foot and held it up for me to see. Blood seeped from the puncture.

"Look at that."

She pointed to one of the trees with black bark, thicker than the rest with it's crooked and bent limbs sprouting the same thorns like an arsenal. "We gotta go around. I can't walk here or I'll get stuck again. The acorns are bad enough but them old thorn trees are killers."

"Which way?" I asked.

"Start going toward your right and around," she said.

I reached out to her.

"Here, take my hand."

She waved my offer away and took a careful step forward, testing her foot gingerly.

"Let's go," she said.

Suddenly, Tony's haunting voice floated through the trees, chilling the hot summer air.

"Dory! Where you at, Dory? I know you here. I've come to take you back where you belong."

His taunting call seemed to be everywhere. A yelp slipped from Dory's lips. She covered her mouth with her hand. Bracing herself against a small tree, she took a deep breath and closed her eyes. I didn't know what to do. Frightened of Tony and unable to help Dory, I felt completely helpless.

"Dory. You know I'm gonna find you."

Frozen where I stood, I couldn't take my eyes off Dory. I waited for her to crumple to the ground. Her breathing came fast and heavy and when her eyes flew open they were dark and void of emotion. She stared right through me.

"Not this time you son-of-a-bitch," she whispered through gritted teeth.

Her hands whipped up her dress, exposing her naked body underneath. Wrapped around her waist was an olive green belt with a large knife secured in a sheaf. She pulled the knife out and held it in her right hand. The left hand reached for me.

"Let's get the hell out of this place," she said.

"What about the thorns?"

"Fuck the thorns."

Grabbing me around the neck, she limped beside me as we started a crooked path to the road. Every time I took a step, Dory hopped forward on her right foot. Teeth clinched, she endured the pain each time she landed on the sharp edges of broken acorns. I stopped once when she cried out but Dory prodded me on. It didn't take us long before I saw the graded surface of the road.

"There it is," I cried.

We'd made it! Dory and I started to laugh as if reaching that road would be the end of our problems. With Dory grasping my shoulder, we began a stumbling run toward our destination. Tony's singsong voice floated from the woods again as we drew closer to the road.

"I hear you, Dory. You better not run from me. You know what'll happen if you do."

Those chilling words only brought us strength and before we realized it, we broke out of the trees and pitched head first into the gully that ran beside the road. My head slammed against a rock and the world began to spin around uncontrollably. My attempts to get up were met by a body that no longer wanted to hear what my mind wanted. I felt hands on my face and at first I thought it was Tony. Dory's voice broke through the fog and her hands rubbed my cheeks.

"Get up, Mac. Ya gotta get up. I lost my knife in that tumble so we have to get out of here."

My head rolled on my shoulders. I blinked my eyes to bring her face into focus. Suddenly, a sharp pain encircled my head and I cried out in pain.

"I told you I find you Dory."

Tony sounded closer now and that realization cleared my head enough that I made a feeble attempt to get to my feet. Dory's hands left my face and I heard her fumbling around in the grass. I was on my back and I slowly turned my head and saw him. He wasn't on us yet, but close enough to scare me to death. A smirk spread across his face as he slowly ambled toward us as though he had all the time in the world.

"You stay back, Tony!" Dory screamed. Her hands continued to paw the ground and I heard the ping of steel hitting rock. "I got a knife."

Tony stopped abruptly. Dory edged back to me and tugged at the front of my shirt to pull me up. I took a deep breath, positioned my hands firmly on the hot rock, and began to push. Slowly, with Dory's help, I raised my body forward until I stood in a crouched position.

"He no man for you, Dory. You better leave him, Dory. He a dead boy," Tony taunted.

Dory's voice was low and pleading. "Come on, Mac. You gotta stand up. We gotta fight him. He'll kill you and take me."

Standing upright shot a piercing pain through my head and I thought I would crumple but Dory caught me. I'd never experienced real terror until I looked into her eyes. The fierceness I'd seen earlier had been replaced with an emptiness that paralyzed me. We stumbled out of the ditch and stood on the road facing Tony. I held my head and Dory held the knife. As if in answer Tony reached into his back pocket and pulled out the slingshot. The sun glinted menacingly off of the bright metal. Tony reached in the bag around his neck, pulled out a rock and placed it in the pocket of the slingshot. He pinched the pocket between his fingers and lifted the slingshot to aim. It seemed to take forever for him to pull the bands of rubber taut. A sly smile crept across his face as he let go and the rock sailed passed my head

"You son of a bitch!" Dory screamed and reached down for rocks of her own to throw.

I held my hands in front of my face for protection. I soon realized that Tony wasn't shooting rocks at us, only me.

"I gonna kill your little friend, Dory. You know you ain't 'posed to have friends."

Tony laughed as he sent rock after rock at me. The missiles flew around my head while I danced like a monkey to avoid getting hit. Tony could have hit me with any of the rocks but he took pleasure in taunting Dory and me. He had to show us that he was in command. A rock hit my chest, spinning me around. Another hit my leg and I crashed to one knee. Dory had become hysterical. Crying and calling Tony every name in the book, I could tell she knew we were losing this battle.

"Dory, you better get back. I gonna get your little boy here."

I realized that he wasn't really using the full force of the slingshot. He kept approaching, a wicked grin on his face. Then like a flipped switch, it all changed. Slowing to a standstill, he pulled out another rock and methodically placed it in the sling. The taunting grin was gone. Tony was deadly serious. His arm lifted, as he pulled the pocket back until it sat just beside his jaw. I heard a twang and the rock hit me on the side of my head. I shot backwards and lay sprawled in the middle of the road.

"Mac!" Dory screamed.

She picked up the knife that lay on the ground and flung it wildly. It was Tony's turn to cry out. I lifted my head and saw him pulling the knife out of his leg. I know now that it didn't go in very deep but it didn't matter. The rage on his face told me that both of us were as good as dead. He rushed us like a mad man. His arms flung out, the knife waving wildly in one hand, and a look of pure rage on his face. My arms covered my head for protection although I knew it wouldn't do any good. Dory draped her body over mine, sobbing uncontrollably.

"I'm sorry, Mac. I'm so sorry," she cried in my ear.

A loud explosion rang in my ears and I heard Tony scream in pain.

"That was only one barrel, Tony Grace. The next one is aimed for your backside and don't think I can't hit you."

Through squinted and teary eyes I saw Aunt Holly standing no more than twenty feet away from Tony, a double barreled twelve-gauge shotgun braced against her shoulder and pointed at Tony's back. I gasped with relief as my head fell back on the hard rock road. I don't really know what happened next it happened so fast. Dory bent over me to brush grit from my face. The shotgun rang out again and there was another scream from Tony. I managed to raise my head far enough to see Tony limping from the edge of the road and disappearing into the trees.

25

Aunt Holly stood over me. The shotgun hung open on one arm and she deftly stuffed two more shells in the barrels. I don't think she had ever looked more beautiful to me. Her hair was pulled back in a ponytail and her face glistened with sweat. One of John's old army t-shirts hung loosely on her shoulders. Her jeans were molded to her legs and stuffed in a pair of dirty and faded cowboy boots.

"There, I've reloaded," she said. "I don't know if Tony will come back or not."

"He always comes back," Dory said more to herself than to us.

Aunt Holly bent down and looked at my head.

"That hurt?" she asked, gently rubbing the gash on my forehead.

I winced and pulled back.

"Some, I guess. I mainly feel dizzy."

"We need to get you to the doctor."

She turned to Dory and her hands started at the top of her head and trailed down her body until she came to Dory's feet.

"My God, little lady, the bottoms of your feet look like ground meat. I don't even want you to walk on them until the doctor sees you."

"I ain't got no money for no doctor," Dory said.

Aunt Holly eyed her for a second. "Have you ever been to a doctor?" Dory shook her head. Aunt Holly patted her cheek and smiled. "We'll work it out. First I have to figure how to get us out of here."

I mumbled, "You walked carrying a shotgun?"

"No, the shotgun belongs to Miss Murphy. I came by to see if she'd seen you. When I spotted Tony, I asked if I could borrow it. I may take it home with me although her buckshot is too small. I doubt if Tony has any to pick out of his sorry butt but it sure got him moving."

At that moment, Miss Murphy came running down the road toward us. Big red roses on her white dress billowed around her slight frame like the wings of some exotic bird. Her oversized sandals slapped the rough road and made her gait awkward while one hand clamped a big straw hat firmly to her head, the brim flapping.

"I called the sheriff," she panted when she reached us. She stared at Dory's feet. "Oh, you poor girl. You need to see a doctor before talking to the sheriff." She turned to Aunt Holly. "Let's pile in my truck and I'll take you to town."

"What about the sheriff?" Aunt Holly asked.

Miss Murphy placed a finger to her puckered lips. "Oh, I forgot about that."

"Maybe he could meet us at the doctor's office," Aunt Holly said.

Miss Murphy owned a 1936 Chevy pickup that had seen better days. It looked like the fenders had more rust than metal and they quivered as she drew along side us. She'd thrown a bunch of old blankets in the truck bed. I crawled in and leaned against the cab while the two women carefully lifted Dory in their arms and placed her on the tailgate. Aunt

Holly jumped in the bed of the truck and scooted Dory up beside me.

"There," Aunt Holly said, slapping her hands together. Miss Murphy handed her the shotgun. She wedged between the two of us and camped the shotgun between her legs. "Let's go," she hollered to Miss Murphy.

The jolt of the truck starting sent my head spinning. Aunt Holly draped an arm around my shoulder and placed an old cotton blanket between my head and the cab. Gently pulling my head to her shoulder, she kissed me. I looked up in her eyes and tried to smile. I felt so safe to be cradled in her arms. I'd thought that Dory and I were dead for sure. Dory sat silently with her hands in her lap. The truck crept onto the main road and started down the hill toward town. It hit me as we reached Mile Branch and started climbing the hill that we had to pass Dory's house. The rocky road bumped us up and down, side to side but I couldn't take my eyes off of Dory. The closer we came to the fork in the road where she lived, the more her eyes became like large saucers. She leaned forward and her hands picked at her dress. Aunt Holly draped her other arm around Dory and pulled her near. Dory resisted at first. She kept her head turned toward the outside and her body was visibly trembling when we reached the top.

"Dory! You come here!"

I turned to see Mrs. Grace run from her house with an angry scowl on her face. Dory buried her head in Aunt Holly's shoulder. Mrs. Grace stood in the middle of the road screeching at Dory until our dust trail obliterated her. I watched for Tony. I didn't see him but like Dory, I felt him. I knew he was close by.

By the time we got to Bolivar my head was throbbing. Dory hadn't moved from Aunt Holly's shoulder since we saw her stepmother. Miss Murphy slammed the truck door shut and rushed into the doctor's office. A minute later she came rushing back and grabbed the edge of the truck bed.

"The doc had to leave to deliver a baby. He has a nurse seeing his patients until he gets back."

Aunt Holly grimaced.

"A nurse? No doctor in Bolivar has a nurse."

"Doctor Jeffers called her in because he knew we were coming."

Aunt Holly untangled herself from Dory and me just as the nurse came out the office door. She was about Aunt Holly's age, and on the stout side. Streaks of gray laced her short, black hair that swept backwards over her ears. I could see a determined look on her face as she approached the truck.

"Let's get everyone inside," she said.

Aunt Holly wouldn't let Dory walk, so Miss Murphy helped her carry Dory inside. The examining room was a table, a glass cabinet filled with bandages, bottles and boxes, and an uncomfortable wooden chair that sat against one wall. The ceiling was high, the window closed, and it was hotter than blue blazes. Since there was only one examining room, Dory and I quietly sat side by side.

"How do you feel?" Aunt Holly asked, her head bobbing between Dory and me.

"Better," I said. "My head still hurts but it doesn't throb as much."

"Okay," Dory whispered.

Aunt Holly put her forefinger under Dory's chin and slowly raised her head up.

"How's your foot? I'm guessing you picked up a thorn or two, eh?"

Dory thought a second before answering.

"Hurts."

"The nurse will be in shortly to fix you both up."

"I'm hot," I said.

"It won't be any better with the window open. There's no circulation in this room. Every patient of Doctor Jeffers says the same thing. I'm only telling you what he'd tell you. I can pull the shade and that might help."

As Aunt Holly pulled the shade down, Dory's hand climbed on top of mine and she squeezed.

"I wish I had a brother like you," she said quietly.

I said, "Maybe you do."

The nurse examined me first because she was afraid that I might have a concussion.

"Does it hurt?" she asked, gingerly touching the large bump forming on my forehead. I winced and pulled away. "Sorry. How many fingers do you see?"

The nurse waved two fingers in front of my face.

"Two."

"Now."

She held up four fingers.

"Four."

"Good. Now follow my finger as I moved it from side to side."

After I followed her finger, she took an instrument and looked in my eyes, then another to look in my ears. Five minutes later she'd finished.

"Is he okay?" asked Aunt Holly.

"I think so. I'd make him rest for the remainder of the day. It's possible he may have a slight concussion. Just watch him and if he shows any signs of sleepiness or..." She pinched me, "...being kind of goofy, call the doctor. He should be back later in the day. I wouldn't be surprised if he didn't slip by your place on his way home, if it isn't too late."

Dory took more time.

"My goodness, child. What happened to the bottom of your feet?" The nurse held one of Dory's feet in her hand and looked from Dory to

Aunt Holly. "I hope they are better than they look. I'm going to need some soap and water to clean them before I can treat."

The nurse left the room and Dory looked over at Aunt Holly.

"She talks funny. She talks like Mac, so she ain't from around here."

Aunt Holly chuckled.

"No, I think she comes from St. Louis. She's the wife of the minister at the Methodist church."

"I don't talk funny," I protested.

"Sure do," Dory replied.

The nurse came back with a metal bowl of soapy water. Sitting on the examining table beside Dory, she began to carefully wash her feet.

"This may hurt a little. I don't think it is as bad as it looks."

Dory leaned back, bracing her arms on the examining table.

"Ow!"

"Sorry, honey. Your feet are really dirty. And the rest of your body could do with a firm washing."

The nurse glanced over at Aunt Holly and gave her a stern look.

"I'm going to give her a shot for infection and then some pills to take. Is she your daughter?"

Aunt Holly looked at Dory out of the corner of her eye.

"Yes, she's my daughter."

A slight smile crept across Dory's face as the nurse pushed her sleeve up, dabbing alcohol for the shot. A bond had been set between my Aunt Holly and Dory.

Miss Murphy had called the sheriff's office and found that Kelly Duncan was south of town investigating some stolen cattle and wouldn't be available until later in the afternoon.

The sheriff had gone to Springfield to a meeting and wouldn't be back until late in the evening, so we headed back home.

25

Aunt Holly suggested that I sit in the cab with Miss Murphy on the way back home. Something told me that she wanted to be alone with Dory. Aunt Holly leaned against the cab, one arm draped around Dory's shoulder. Dory stared out the back of the truck bed while Aunt Holly laughed and talked as if Dory was her best friend--or daughter. We didn't take the same route back home so we didn't have to pass Dory's house and her step mom again. Miss Murphy chattered about Harold but my mind kept returning to the day's events. From the moment I first laid eyes on Tony he frightened me. After today's events, I was afraid for my life and I didn't know what to do. I felt uneasy about Aunt Holly handling this situation. I felt my only safety lay with John. Aunt Holly was a strong woman in more than one way but I didn't believe she could handle Tony. This exciting adventure that had kept my mind off of my ailing father had suddenly turned ugly--and deadly.

The truck pulled in the driveway; it felt good to be home. Stopping beside the house, we clamored out of the truck and headed for the porch.

Aunt Holly entered first.

"This house is sweltering. You all open the windows and I'll get the ice tea out of the icebox."

Miss Murphy turned on the ceiling fan in the kitchen. I threw open a window in the living room and turned to find Dory standing at the front door, her hands pressed against the screen as if ready to escape at any moment.

I waved at her and said, "Dory, come on in or every fly in Polk County is going to make his home in this living room."

She edged into the room until the screen door closed behind her. Her eyes on the floor, a hand carelessly played with a strand of hair that fell across her face.

"Don't be afraid child. Come on in."

Miss Murphy slid an arm through Dory's and led her into the living room. Dory Grace, the toughest girl I'd ever know in my entire life looked like a lost child. As Miss Murphy drew her to the kitchen, Dory's eyes focused on the family pictures that hung on the wall. Her fingers traced along the arm of the sofa as if she'd walked into a palace of some king. I had never seen anyone marvel at ordinary furniture, as Dory did that day. Miss Murphy led her to the kitchen table and pulled out a chair for her. As I look back, I think the trauma of the last few days had finally started to affect Dory. On Monday, when we first met, she had told me that she wanted to die. I believe she felt that death was her only escape from her physical and emotional prison. Once the sheriff had gone after Tony, Dory had seen a chance for freedom. Rid of Tony, she could find a way to get away from her stepmother. Now Tony had returned to her life, bigger and more bruising than ever. I couldn't imagine what was running through her head after our narrow escape earlier that day. I know that I felt like a hollow shell, frightened even of my own shadow.

"What is this?" Miss Murphy picked up a folded sheet of paper from the kitchen table. "Holly's name is on it."

I took the paper out of her hand.

"John wrote this."

"What is it?" Aunt Holly asked as she entered with the ice tea on a tray.

I said, "A note from Uncle John."

Aunt Holly sat the tray down and took the note. She flipped it open and kept adjusting the paper so she could read it.

"Between his small scrawl and my need of glasses, I can hardly read this."

"I'll read it," I offered.

Aunt Holly reached over and pinched my nose.

"And what if it has sweet nothings that are only for me?"

Aunt Holly focused on the lined stationary. The note was short. The smile faded and Aunt Holly's face became solemn.

"What is it, Holly?" asked Miss Murphy.

Aunt Holly's hands dropped to her side and the note fluttered to the floor. I stooped and picked it up and read the small handwriting.

George Baker is ill and couldn't go to the highway meeting in Jefferson City. I am to take his place. Be back Saturday night or Sunday morning. I'll call later.

My eyes slowly rose to meet Aunt Holly. She took the note from my hand and for the first time in my life I saw fear in my Aunt Holly's eyes.

"We'll be fine," she whispered. "We'll be fine."

Miss Murphy laid a hand on Holly's shoulder. "Why don't you try and call him, dear. Explain what has happened today. I know that John would hurry back to be with you."

Our attention was diverted by the sound of a truck coming up the driveway. Kelly Duncan pulled up in front of the house and came to a screeching stop. He jumped out of the truck, pushed his hat back on his head, and tugged up his pants. For a fleeting moment I thought Kelly could protect us but I wasn't sure he was a match for Tony Grace. Standing there in front of the house adjusting his clothes, he reminded me of my older brother getting ready to go out on a date. Aunt Holly ran out the front screen door to stop a few feet from him. Kelly was so surprised he took two steps back and bumped into his truck.

"We had a run-in with Tony."

Kelly stood back up.

"Tell me what happened."

Aunt Holly brushed her hair out of her eyes and began to describe what had happened earlier on the road. Kelly had to stop her for a second while he grabbed a Big Chief tablet from the front seat to take notes.

"Now start all over and go slow," he said.

Aunt Holly took a deep breath and started all over. She had to stop every once in a while to allow Kelly to catch up. Finally he licked the pencil's lead point and entered the last period with flair.

"That's attempted murder, isn't it?" Miss Murphy asked.

"Yes, ma'am. That is attempted murder. Where's John?"

"He had to go to Jefferson City to a meeting," Aunt Holly explained.

Kelly grimaced. He walked back to the truck bed where he kept an old trunk. He lifted the trunk lid and pulled out a cut-off broomstick.

"I'd keep the doors and windows locked. Sleep in the living room and crack one window and let the attic fan do its job. Use this broomstick so he can't lift the window. Does John have a gun?" The expression on Kelly Duncan's face was serious as he handed the cut-off broomstick to Aunt Holly. "I'll inform the neighbors to keep a look out. We don't have anyone patrolling the county at night, just someone on the desk."

"That don't seem right," Miss Murphy grumbled.

Kelly Duncan started to explain. "The county..."

"That's okay, Kelly, we understand." Aunt Holly laid a hand on his shoulder and looked at the fading light. "We'd better get started if we are going to do what Kelly advised."

Dory inched closer to me and grabbed my hand. Her whole body shook and her blue eyes were wide as saucers.

"It's going to be alright," I said.

She cocked her head and gazed at me as if I was crazy. "You don't understand Tony. None of us are okay."

Kelly reached in his pocket for his keys. "I'd like to stay, Holly, but I have to get back to town. I'm on duty tonight."

"Okay, Kelly. Could you follow Miss Murphy back to her place on your way?"

"I not going nowhere," Miss Murphy growled.

26

I awoke with a start. Rising up on my elbows to get my bearings, I saw Miss Murphy sprawled on the sofa, snoring. Dory had curled up in John's chair with the blanket over her head. I'd slept on a pallet on the floor. Scooter must have climbed out of his box because he was snuggled against my leg. The sun had just begun to slip in the east window of the living room, filling the room with a golden sheen. Although the house was literally shut up, I was so tired that I hadn't been uncomfortable last night. I sat up and stretched.

"Good morning."

The words were soft and comforting. I rolled over and found Aunt Holly sitting in a kitchen chair in front of the open window, the shotgun cradled in her lap. A golden halo circled her head but her face lay hidden in the shadows of the morning.

"Have you been up all night?" I asked.

She rose and held the shotgun across her chest. The chair creaked and I heard an audible sigh slip from her lips. She rolled her shoulders and twisted her body to work the kinks out.

"I couldn't sleep. I'll take a nap later today."

"Did you hear anything?"

"No, not really. When you are frightened you tend to hear a lot of things that aren't really there."

"Were you scared," I asked.

"Still am," she responded.

I could make out the faint smile on her face.

I scrambled out of the pallet and rushed to throw my arms around her. I pushed my body against the hard metal of the shotgun but I pushed my head harder into the soft swell of her breasts. I clung tightly to her in hopes that all of this would go away.

"I'm scared, too," I whispered.

Aunt Holly pulled me away from her and bent down until our noses almost touched.

"Nothing is going to happen to you--I promise. You hear me? We are going to be all right. Now, you go get washed up and help me with breakfast."

"Okay," I said, stumbling backward and looking around to see if Dory was awake. She still slept soundly. "I feel better now that it's daytime."

I walked toward the bathroom, passing Dory in the chair. The blanket had slipped down revealing an old Raggedy Ann doll clutched in her arms. Aunt Holly had made the doll and kept it on an old wooden milk bucket next to the chair. Dory gritted her teeth and her eyelids, although closed, fluttered like a moth trapped on the wrong side of a screen door. I glanced back at Aunt Holly.

"I thought she needed it. How's your head?"

"It hurts," I said, carefully rubbing the large bump that now adorned my forehead.

"You were lucky. If you hadn't turned, it could have killed you."

"Really? You didn't tell me that."

"I didn't want to scare you. You seem okay this morning. No headaches? Dizziness?"

I thought for a second.

"Kind of a headache. I can't explain it. First my ribs and now my head. You'd think I'd hurt more but I don't."

"Too much on your mind makes you forget some things. Now, go wash up and help me fix breakfast."

The house was stuffy, the air stagnant, and it was going to get worse later in the day. I looked out the bathroom window and saw that Aunt Holly had nailed the windows shut. It was strange how I was so frightened last night and afraid to go to sleep but failed to hear Aunt Holly hammering. My eyes searched the side yard and the woods beyond for any signs that Tony was there--or had been there. My skin crawled with all the horrors of the unknown. It was almost worse not knowing than seeing some sign that he was watching us.

I heard Miss Murphy talking to Aunt Holly. I wet a washrag and wiped my face and underarms. The Mennen stick deodorant was in the medicine cabinet and I gave my underarms a swipe.

"You going to be much longer?" Miss Murphy shouted. "Some of us old people have to go to the bathroom first thing in the morning and I refuse to go outside."

I started and knocked a can of shaving cream on the floor. I picked it up and answered, "Coming right out."

Miss Murphy slid past me and closed the bathroom door. I heard the toilet seat bang against the tank. Dory sat up in the chair and rocked back and forth, the Raggedy Ann still clutched to her chest. The events of the past two-day had painted dark circles under lifeless eyes. She didn't look up when I entered and when I walked over to her I could see that her lower lip trembled.

"You okay?" I asked.

Dory continued to rock back and forth. Her eyes stared straight ahead and when she answered, her voice was a soft monotone.

"He's out there."

"How do you know?" I asked, feeling the goose pimples raise on my arms.

"I always know," she said, falling back into the chair. "Remember when we were crossing the wheat field yesterday? I knew then. Tony has a magic, but it's a bad magic, that latches on to you and doesn't let go. Tony will follow me to the end of time and back. He thinks I'm his."

"We're going to win."

She looked up at me. Tears rolled down her cheeks. A trembling hand reached out for mine and squeezed it so tight it hurt.

"I almost got you killed yesterday."

"You, too," I said.

"I'm sorry."

"Don't be. It isn't your fault," I said.

Dory pulled on my hand until our foreheads touched.

"He's out there. I know it."

I didn't say anything for a second. Her breath was hot on my face and her eyes searched mine for some reassurance I couldn't give. My eyes wandered to the one window in the living room that was open; a mere three or four inches for air. I imagined Tony sitting just inside the tree line, perhaps sitting in the treetops, watching and waiting for the right moment. The thought petrified me because that meant that Tony might make it in the house. I had no doubt about that. I heard Aunt Holly rummaging around in the kitchen and wondered how she could stand up to

Tony. She'd taken him by surprise yesterday but what could she do when Tony was in control, and Tony was in control at the moment. Why else did we all sleep in one room with all the windows closed? If John were here things would be different. John could protect us. Tony would back down if he saw John here, or so I thought. My eyes fell back on Dory, nervously biting her lip.

"Are you sure he's here?" I asked.

"I lived with Tony for the past six years. I knows how he thinks, how he moves, and feels."

I stood up, shifting nervously back and forth.

"What is he feeling right now?"

Her dull eyes stared up at me like I was stupid.

"How do you think he feels? He hates us. He hates us all and he wants to strike out and hurt us."

"Would he kill us?"

She gave a snort and shook her head.

"Tony is capable of anything. Why do you even ask that? He almost killed you yesterday."

"Would he kill you?" I asked, leaning on the arms of the chair and staring Dory straight in the face.

"I'm afraid he won't," she said softly and curled back up in the chair with the Raggedy Ann.

"It's hard for me to understand what makes him do what he does. It's like he owns you."

Dory thought a second before she replied.

"He just don't know any better. It just his way."

"Mac, come in here. I need some help."

"Coming, Aunt Holly." I reached out and touched Dory's shoulder. "I still say we're going to beat Tony."

Dory didn't answer.

Aunt Holly leaned against the kitchen counter, her face grim. She motioned for me to be quiet. I stopped in front of her and waited. It took her a couple of seconds before she could speak.

"Mac, I don't know what's going to happen with Tony. He reminds me of a caged animal that broke free. He's apt to do anything and to hell with the consequences."

"You mean hurt us?" I asked.

She nodded. "Yes, I mean he'll hurt us. I'm afraid for Dory. I'm afraid for you. And, I'm afraid for Miss Murphy. I'm afraid if I send her back home he will break in her house and hurt her... maybe even kill her." She was quiet to let that sink in my head. "I can't let that happen to any of you."

"What are you going to do?"

Aunt Holly grabbed my shoulders and her fingers dug in so hard I winced.

"I want the three of you to leave while I wait for John."

"But where will we go? Tony will follow us. Dory already said that. My dad is sick so we can't go to Kansas City. Dory and Miss Murphy have no relatives."

Aunt Holly stood up and snapped her fingers.

"That's it!" A smile spread across her face. "Miss Murphy has a cousin in St. Louis. We can get you all on the bus later this morning and send you to stay with her cousin for the weekend."

Aunt Holly ran from the kitchen to find Miss Murphy who'd just come out of the bathroom. I didn't listen to any of the muffled conversation because I didn't think it'd work. The bus had to take us to Springfield where we'd transfer and take Highway 66 on another bus to St. Louis. We wouldn't arrive in St. Louis until late at night. By the time we got there it would almost be time to turn around and come back home. I took a glass from the cabinet and went to the sink to get a drink. I tipped the glass back and that's when I saw a retreating foot disappear behind the tool shed. It took me a minute to process what I'd just seen. Closing my eyes, I attempted to play the scene again in my mind. Recreating a past moment in your mind is difficult if you're not prepared. Was the person wearing jeans or cotton pants? Were those boots or high-top tennis shoes? The only thing I was sure of was that it was a boy and I knew who it was. I ran into the living room and saw that Miss Murphy wasn't entirely sold on Aunt Holly's idea.

"I don't know if Elizabeth can do it," she said. "She hasn't been feeling too well lately. This hot weather has been awfully hard on her."

"Aunt Holly..." I interrupted.

"Wait a minute, Mac. Miss Murphy, we can't leave these children here with this maniac running loose."

Dory hadn't moved in the chair. In fact, the more Aunt Holly talked, the tighter she curled into a ball.

"I saw him!" I blurted out.

Dory's head ducked deeper into the cushion of the chair. Miss Murphy stood with her mouth open as if she wanted to speak but couldn't. Aunt Holly stared at me through narrowed eyes considering my words. I waited but time stood still in that moment. The school clock in the kitchen ticked in an off-key harmony with the attic fan whirring over our heads.

Aunt Holly was the first to recover. Her hands nervously brushed at the front of her blouse and her tired eyes widened in determination.

"Where did you see him?" she asked.

I took a deep breath and pointed toward the kitchen.

"Through the kitchen window just now. He was sneaking behind the tool shed."

"Did you see his face?" Aunt Holly asked.

I hesitated.

"No. Just his leg."

Aunt Holly placed her hands on my shoulders and bent over until her eyes were level with mine. She asked, "Just what did you see, Mac?"

I took another deep breath.

"I was looking out the kitchen window. I don't know if I heard a noise but I turned my head and saw someone disappear behind the tool shed."

Aunt Holly straightened up, dropping her hands to her sides.

"I told you he would come back," Dory moaned. We turned to see Dory sitting up in the chair, the doll now on the floor. "I let myself think I could get away. I should have known better."

Dory bit her lower lip, placed her trembling hands in her lap and stared straight ahead.

Miss Murphy placed a hand on her head.

"Child, we don't know if that was Tony. Larry Thomas lives down the road and he's always chasing his dog Luther. It probably was Larry. I catch him at my place chasing after that dog all the time. It's an almost daily occurrence."

That didn't seem to placate Dory. Her body began to rock back and forth again. Her hands rolled around in her lap. I didn't know this Dory Grace. Gone was the cockiness, that glibness. As I look back, I think she had started to change when she saw her stepmother. Suddenly it hit me. Before that moment, Dory had been able to slip in and out of sight. Avoiding Tony had been a game, a game she didn't want to play but she had become very adroit at it. Now he had her trapped. What little control she'd had earlier was gone.

"I knew I shouldn't come here!" she shouted, pointing an accusatory finger at me. "I trusted you and now he'll kill us all."

Aunt Holly ran to her and cradled Dory in her arms.

"Shush, child. Nothing is going to happen to any of us. I promise you that."

Dory buried her face in the nap of Aunt Holly's neck and sobbed uncontrollably. This was the same girl that just a few days earlier had boasted about dying. I have learned since then that the death mask we all wear on the backs of our heads continually changes as we meet different challenges. Dory's death mask had changed to one of fear. Many times in life, people aren't afraid of death. It's just what they have to go through to get there. Maybe that is what Dory was afraid of that Friday morning.

The morning dragged on and the house became almost unbearable. Usually the front and back doors were open along with every window in the house. Aunt Holly spent the morning trying to get in touch with John but Bolivar still had a live operator who had to make the phone call to Jefferson City. She could make the call but we didn't really know where John's meeting was being held. Sometimes it was in a state office building and sometimes they met off-site but Aunt Holly didn't know who, what, or where about the meeting. The operator didn't have time to call all over Jefferson City looking for John. As the sun lifted higher in the sky, the more irritable everyone had become. Scooter didn't help, either. He was hot and wanted outside every five minutes. I wanted to take him outside but Aunt Holly wouldn't allow it.

"Not until we know," she said.

Around eleven o'clock we heard the roar of a car pulling into the driveway and everyone assumed it was John. We rushed to the window to see Kelly Duncan pull up in front of the house and stop. He was driving a 1936 Ford coupe, one of two official police cars owned by the sheriff's office. He had changed caps but the jeans and shirt looked the same. I wondered why they didn't have uniforms like the police did in the city. He started for the front door, then stopped and went back to the car to fetch a small, white envelope. A smile spread across his face as he knocked on the front door.

"Come in, come in," Miss Murphy said, opening the door.

Kelly stepped in and stopped.

"Wow, I thought it was getting hot outside. It's like an oven in here."

"Mac thought he saw Tony this morning dodging behind the tool shed," Aunt Holly explained.

"Couldn't have," Kelly replied. "Ben Kirkpatrick caught him trying to steal some milk out of his milk house last night. Trained a 12-gauge at him while his wife called our office. I went out and picked him up myself. I left the jail early this morning and he was still tucked in tight. I have to check on some dealings up north near Hickory County but I should be back late this afternoon. You're safe."

Dory popped out of the chair and grabbed my arm.

"We're safe," she whimpered.

"Did you hear that, Dory? He's in jail. You're safe. No reason to be sad."

"Let's open up this house," Miss Murphy growled and shuffled around the room throwing open the windows.

Kelly stretched out his hand that held the small envelope.

"And I brought this out to you, Holly. Roy McManus gave it to me since his mail route hits you late in the day. He thought it might be important since it was from Kansas City."

Aunt Holly looked at me with apprehension. She tore off one end of the envelope and pulled out lined stationary. I recognized my mom's small handwriting. The envelope fluttered to the ground as her lips slowly moved as she read. She flipped the letter over to the other side and she gave me a big grin.

"He's going to be okay," she said.

"Does this mean I get to go back home?"

Aunt Holly laughed.

"No. Your mom said that you have to stay the summer and give your dad time to get his strength back. He needs his rest, Mac. Anyway, I'm not ready to let loose of you."

I started to cry knowing that my dad would be okay. Dory squeezed my arm and Aunt Holly gave me a hug. That was one thing I will always remember about Aunt Holly. I think she looked at hugs like some people think of medicine. Aunt Holly had wrapped her arms around Dory, too. Squeezing us together until I started to laugh. The frustrations of the past twenty-four hours were released and we were all becoming giddy.

Miss Murphy clapped her hands together.

"This means we can go to the ice cream social tonight."

27

Aunt Holly sat in a rocking chair on the front porch, busily fanning herself with a fan from the local funeral parlor. I had only gone to one funeral in my young life. My grandfather had died and my family had made the four-hour trip from Kansas City. It was September but still hot. There were ceiling fans moving hot air. As you entered, a somber looking man in a dark suit handed you a fan with a picture of Jesus rising into heaven on one side and the name of the funeral home on the other.

"Do you want a fan?" she asked. She'd noticed me eyeing hers.

"No, I'm fine. Is that fan from grandfather's funeral?"

"I don't know. That was a long time ago and you still remember coming down for the funeral? You couldn't have been more than four or five."

"I was six," I answered.

"Still, that was a long time ago."

We were silent for a second. I think we were trying to get our balance. At least that is what my father would say. Sometimes things happen in life that throw your life off balance. A person just needs to sit a spell and let things right on their own, he would say. I missed my father. It was in the short moment of reflection that I realized what he'd given me. True, he wasn't an affectionate man. There were very few hugs in my life and men didn't kiss. The very things that a young man needed I didn't get. There were other things I received that were just as valuable like my father's ability to show patience and listen. He never told me how to do things but gave me options. He gave me a solid foundation for life. I wondered if Dory's father had lived if she would have had a solid foundation. I didn't think so because he married Tony's mother.

"I'm glad that I get to stay the summer with you," I said.

Aunt Holly gave me a surprised look.

"Well, I'm glad, too. I've enjoyed having you around the house."

Scooter woke up and started whimpering in his box. I reached down and picked him up.

"You'd better put him out on the grass so he can pee. He's been asleep all morning."

I walked out into the yard and sat him down. He immediately began sniffing for a choice spot.

"He's okay, don't you think?" I asked.

"Honey, he's had more excitement and travels in one week than most dogs get in a lifetime."

"Boy, that's the truth."

Dory came to the screen door.

"I took a bath," she said.

Aunt Holly waved an arm for her to come outside.

"Come join us. We're just taking it easy."

Dory came out and plopped down on the concrete porch beside Aunt Holly. It was obvious that the two were becoming close. It also gave me a twinge of jealousy. Although I'd suggested that Dory come and stay with Aunt Holly, I still wanted to be first in Aunt Holly's eyes. Dory sat on the porch, her arms wrapped around her knees as usual, staring up at Aunt Holly as if she were an angel.

"I've got some lavender in my bedroom you can splash on after your bath. Would you like to do that?" Holly asked as she gently squeezed Dory's arm.

"I ain't never wore anything like that," Dory answered.

"We'll go inside in a minute and put some on for you. Okay?"

Dory shook her head and then fell back against Aunt Holly's arm and closed her eyes.

"You ever want kids, Holly?" she asked.

Aunt Holly placed the fan in her lap. With a far away look on her face she simply nodded.

"You can't have children. Right, Aunt Holly?"

Immediately I regretted that statement. I learned much later in life that Aunt Holly considered that her biggest failure - her inability to give John a son or a daughter. It was always the wife's fault back then, never the man's. The hurt expression on her face made me wish I'd kept my mouth shut.

"No, John and I can't have children," she said softly.

"Your a good mom."

Dory's soothing voice brought a smile to Aunt Holly's face. She reached down and stroked Dory's wet hair.

"You want me to brush your hair?" Aunt Holly asked. Dory eagerly nodded her head. "Go into my bedroom and you'll find a brush on my dresser next to the window. Get it and we'll see about getting some tangles out."

I returned to my rocking chair with Scooter in my arms.

"I'm sorry I blurted that out, Aunt Holly."

"Never mind. It's the truth. I just don't like to hear it, okay?"

"Did you hear from John?" I asked, changing the subject.

She shook her head.

"Gladys said she'd try and track him down. She did find out what hotel they were staying at, so she left a message for him to call."

"Do you really think they'll keep Tony in jail?"

Aunt Holly closed her eyes and sighed.

"I certainly hope so."

Dory came bouncing out the front door and handed the brush to Aunt Holly. I decided that it was time I go fishing.

"I'm going to leave Scooter here. I think he needs to rest instead of chasing grasshoppers."

Dory giggled like a small girl. She was almost giddy with relief and excitement. For the first time in years I believe she felt safe. Sitting on the porch, she leaned her head back and closed her eyes as Aunt Holly stroked her hair with the brush. It was time for me to go.

I retrieved the fishing pole from the tool shed. The door creaked and I expected Tony to leap out at me. The sun slipped through the cracks in the walls exposing a thin layer of dust floating in the air. I chose the rod Aunt Holly had bought for me a couple of summers ago. I picked up the tackle box and started to leave when I heard a loud crash behind me. My heart skipped a beat. I dropped the rod and tackle box and immediately tripped on something soft that sent my head tumbling into the doorframe. I fell to the ground, ignoring the pain, and rolled over to avoid Tony's boot. That's when I saw the tail of the raccoon dodge around the corner of the tool shed.

I sighed in relief and rubbed my head.

I scrambled to my feet and brushed myself off. My fishing pole and tackle box in hand, I headed for the pond. Even though I knew Tony was in jail, I still feared him. I wondered if I would ever shake that fear. Would Dory get over her fear of Tony? His obsession with Dory was beyond anything that my young mind could understand. It was like he needed her. There was certainly no one else in his life but his mother. Who knows what that relationship was like? An outcast from society and unable to adapt, he probably saw Dory in his depraved mind as his only human contact. And he needed to control that contact. He needed her and the fact that she didn't reciprocate enraged him.

I shuddered at the thought.

The old weeping willow provided some relief from the sun. My head still held the dull ache from slamming against the doorframe. Digging through the bait can I pulled out a fat worm that was mostly mushy. Securing it to the hook, I tossed my line in the water and waited. The bobber sent initial waves across the calm water, and then it settled in for the long wait. The quiet was discomforting. Used to the brazen blast of horns and roaring engines of city life, I only heard the occasional tractor or truck. At night it became drop dead silence except for frogs and other insects. Sitting beside the pond I suddenly felt vulnerable. If something happened to me, no one would know until it was too late. Despite those thoughts, I soon dozed off.

I awoke to the sound of someone sitting down beside me. I jerked up into a sitting position to find Dory picking up a small rock and throwing it at my bobber.

"Hey, you'll scare the fish," I exclaimed.

"You ain't catching nothin'," she said, picking up another rock and tossing it at the bobber again.

"Where's Aunt Holly?"

"She said she had some things to do for the ice cream social tonight, so I decided to join you."

Dory grabbed another rock and examined it for a second before she tossed it into the pond.

"You okay?" I asked.

She averted looking at me. Her eyes followed the gravel road that led down to Mile Branch and to her small sandstone house. You could see the roof and chimney from where we sat but trees hid the house. Her hand reached for another rock to toss, and then another. I reached out to stop her but she fought me off and continued to throw stones at nothing in particular. Years of frustration, fear, and anxiety had erupted inside her and she couldn't stop until it all came out.

"I hate him! I hate him! I hate him!" she screamed.

Dory stood up, stamped her feet, and cried uncontrollably until, finally exhausted, she fell backward and covered her face. Nothing in my past had taught me how to handle this situation. I reached out to comfort her but she brushed my hand away--so I just sat and waited and wondered what all Tony had done to Dory. The question had always been circling in the back of my mind but I was afraid to ask. I'd seen the bruises and witnessed how he treated her. I turned to say something and that's when I saw Aunt Holly running toward us.

"What's wrong?" she gasped.

"I don't know," I lied. "She started throwing rocks and yelling how she hated Tony."

Dory's hands were clamped on her face like a locked iron gate. Aunt Holly placed her hands on Dory's and gently spoke to her.

"Come on, child. Holly wants to help, but I can't help unless you let me in."

I backed up and leaned against the willow tree and watched.

"I love you, Dory. You can't shut me out. I'm here for you. You can stay with John and me for as long as you want. That would make us so happy."

Slowly the hands moved and Dory gave a big sob and reached for Aunt Holly. Every once in a while Aunt Holly would look at me and I'd freeze. I didn't know what to do.

"Do you really love me?" Dory asked through sobs.

"Yes I do, honey. I surely do."

Dory pulled away and kept Aunt Holly at arms length.

"How can you love me? You don't even know me."

"Sometimes you just know. A connection is made, and you know it was meant to be. Riding in the truck with you yesterday was all I needed. Coming home with my arm around you, I knew then that I couldn't let you go."

"Really?"

"Really," Aunt Holly answered and pulled Dory into her arms.

28

I don't know which of was more excited about the ice cream social. Miss Murphy, Aunt Holly, and Dory spent the rest of the afternoon getting everything together. Who knew you had to have bowls, spoons, and napkins. Miss Murphy came by with an armload of napkins that were just old towels she'd torn into squares. There was a bounce in their walk and Miss Murphy even made a very poor attempt to hum in harmony with Aunt Holly. Miss Murphy left to get ready for the evening. I went to the bookcase and found something to read. Instead of reading the book, I sat down on the floor and stared at my reflection in the glass door of the bookcase. For me, something was wrong. It had nagged at me all day but I couldn't put my finger on it. There was something about the leg disappearing around the tool shed this morning. It wasn't some kid that lived down the road chasing his dog: it was Tony. I was certain, even if all I saw was a leg wearing jeans and tennis shoes. There was nothing I could say because Kelly said they'd caught Tony and he was locked up in the county jail. They could think what they wanted but my gut told me different. The only problem with my "gut" feeling was why didn't he come after Dory? He could have easily done anything he wanted to us. I didn't want to tell Dory because she was so happy thinking Tony was in jail.

I escaped to the front porch with Scooter, an apple, and a book. Scooter sat in my lap and snapped at flies. Frustrated, he finally laid his head down and fell asleep. I leisurely ate the apple and skimmed through The Works of Robert Lewis Stevenson, and began to read Kidnapped. Finished with the apple, I tossed it out in the yard. I'd just started to get into the book when Dory skipped out the front door. I don't think I'd ever seen her happier.

With a playful look on her face, she asked, "Whatcha doing?"

Scooter woke up at the sound of her voice. He whined and she reached down to pick him up.

"Reading," I replied, not daring to look up because I was afraid that she could tell something was wrong. There was no use getting her upset when I couldn't prove anything. She paused for a second, then sat on the porch in front of me and scratched Scooter's head.

"You excited about the ice cream social?"

I shrugged and kept reading. "I guess."

"I'm so happy. I ain't never been to an ice cream social before." She paused and her face became draped in sadness. "I ain't been much any-where before."

"Uh-huh."

Dory reached up and pushed the book down into my lap.

"What's wrong? Why don't you talk to me?"

Her eyes could penetrate Fort Knox so I cast my eyes down to my lap.

"I don't know. So much has happened this week. I guess I'm just tired."

I smiled at her. Dory was so enthralled by her newfound freedom she took what I said at face value.

"I know what you mean. Holly said I should take a nap because I didn't sleep good last night."

I nodded and closed my book.

"I guess you feel better knowing Tony is in jail." A slight nod was her silent reply. "He is one weird guy."

"You don't know it all," she replied, holding Scooter straight up in the air. She giggled softly at the limp puppy.

"He didn't hurt you, did he?"

Dory frowned and her eyes flashed.

"You seen my bruises. That's a stupid question!"

My hands nervously opened and closed the book in my lap. A noisy crow landed in the gravel drive and picked greedily at the apple core. I narrowed my eyes like I was focusing all of my attention on that old crow.

"Did he ever kiss you... and stuff?"

Dory recoiled like I'd hit her.

"God, no! Are you crazy?"

I knew from our past history that I needed to get off the subject.

"I just wondered. I'm glad he's in jail, too. I have never been so afraid of someone in my life."

She carefully placed Scooter by her side and dusted off her lap before she stood up. "What made you ask me that?"

"I don't know. Just forget it. I didn't mean anything by it."

She looked at me as tears trickled down her face. White with anger, she spoke through clinched teeth, "He didn't want my body, you fool! He wanted my essence. He wanted my life." She wiped the tears away with the back of one hand. "I was his possession... his slave. Nothing more."

The door slammed behind her as she ran into the house crying. Dory shut herself in until it was time to go to the ice cream social. I remained on the porch but every once in a while Aunt Holly would stick her head out the screen door and give me a look that meant I should do something, but I didn't know what to do. I only had a brother and my experience around girls was very limited outside of school. I don't think that lack of experience made any difference to Aunt Holly or Dory. I felt like I'd become the enemy along with Tony.

At five-forty Miss Murphy came walking up the driveway. A large feedbag was folded under one arm and a large purse hung over her shoulder. I think that was the first time I'd seen Miss Murphy without a hat of some kind perched on her head. Long gray hair hung to her shoulders and a large white barrette held her hair out of her face. Her yellow dress had bright orange flowers and small hummingbirds on it. She waved as she neared the porch.

"You ready for the big shindig?"

"I guess. You look really nice tonight, Miss Murphy."

"I've had this thing for years but I've never worn it. Thought I'd dig it out and wear it tonight. Looks bright and cheery, don't it?"

She spread the dress with her hands and gave a little bow.

"It looks very cheery," I said.

Aunt Holly came out of the front door and placed her hands on her hips.

"I guess you're going to be the queen of the ball tonight."

"I told Mac that I thought I needed to wear something cheery after all we went through yesterday."

Aunt Holly stepped off the porch and walked around Miss Murphy appraisingly.

"You look mighty fine."

Miss Murphy gave another short curtsey and giggled like a schoolgirl. Aunt Holly glanced at me and jerked her head toward the door.

"I think you need to go get Dory."

"Yes, ma'am." I took a step toward the door and stopped to face Aunt Holly. "I didn't mean anything."

"Just go," she said, and she cocked one eyebrow to emphasize what she expected of me.

"What's going on?" Miss Murphy asked. "Is something wrong with Dory?"

Aunt Holly placed her arm around Miss Murphy's shoulders. "No, she's fine. Why don't you and I sit on the porch for minute before we get the ice cream out."

The house was quiet. Dory wasn't in the living room or kitchen. I checked the back porch and that left only the bedrooms. I found her curled up on Aunt Holly's bed. The room was hot and stuffy even with the window open. The floor creaked as I approached the bed and Dory looked at me over her shoulder.

"I didn't mean anything," I said before she could talk. A shrug of the shoulders was her only reply. "We need to talk."

"What for?"

"Because we're friends. Maybe more than friends."

Quiet for a second, she responded in a low voice. "Does everybody think Tony did bad things to me?"

"I don't know. You know I would never hurt you on purpose. Come on. Get up. We need to help Aunt Holly with the ice cream."

She rolled over to face me. "I'd have killed myself if Tony had touched me like you think."

"I know. My mom use to tell my brother he needed to take his foot out of his mouth before he spoke. I guess it kind of runs in my family."

Dory giggled, wiped her runny nose on the back of her hand, and bounced off the bed. She wound her arms around me and held me so tight I fought for air. The smell of Aunt Holly's lavender perfume tickled my nose and I noticed that Dory's hair was clean. I stood limp-armed for a second before my arms encircled her. Baseball, the ice cream social, Tony, my father, and everything else in the world was forgotten in that moment. My feet were inches above the floor as I floated in a dream world that I didn't want to end.

29

Aunt Holly wouldn't let me take Scooter to the ice cream social. He whined and clawed at his box as we shut the front door. It wouldn't be long before the box would be too small for him. I wondered what we'd do with him then when we left. As we followed the path to the schoolhouse, the pungent smell of smoke still lingered in the air. I noticed for the first time that the nearer we approached the schoolhouse, the leaves on the trees drooped from the heat of the fire. Dory walked holding Aunt Holly's hand while Miss Murphy and I each carried a cardboard box with ice cream canisters. We walked into the schoolyard to find tables and chairs filling the front yard and people were busy unloading cars. In the center of the schoolyard sat a metal water trough filled with ice. Ice cream canisters sat to one side of the table. A string of multi-colored light bulbs had been strung from a utility pole to a tree by the charred remains of the schoolhouse.

Stopping to admire the lights and the chairs and tables, Miss Murphy whispered, "Well, I'll be."

"It's beautiful!" Dory squeezed Aunt Holly's hand.

"I'm amazed they pulled it off," said Aunt Holly.

"This is our farewell to the school," said Miss Murphy.

I didn't say anything. I guess coming from Kansas City it was going to take more than tables and a string of light bulbs to impress me. There were cars parked beside the road. Some had pulled into the schoolyard to provide light later in the evening.

"What do you do at an ice cream social?" Dory asked.

Aunt Holly was taking the ice cream canisters out of the boxes and pushing them down into the ice.

"Lots of things. You just don't eat ice cream. We have three-legged races, bag races, and there will be music."

"Oh, that sounds like so much fun."

"It is," Aunt Holly answered.

Dory clapped her hands in anticipation. She continued to reveal different sides of herself. One minute she clapped her hands as a small child would. The next minute she's throwing a knife at her stepbrother. I realize now that the lack of continuity in her young life meant she had no foundation on which to build her life. She sailed through life like a rudderless sailboat, reacting to the different winds as she drifted. I felt like I was in the midst of someone growing up very fast now that she was free.

Miss Murphy found a table near the trough, so we were one of the first to be served ice cream. Men and women carried the ice cream canisters and went around to each table to serve it. I had a scoop of vanilla and strawberry while Dory had strawberry and chocolate. I remembered how earlier in the week she had devoured my ice cream cone like she'd never eaten one before. I watched her tonight, anticipating smears of chocolate all over her face. Her eyes never left Aunt Holly. When Aunt Holly took a bite of ice cream, Dory took a bite of ice cream. Dory had finally found someone to model her behavior after.

Aunt Holly stood up and reached for the dirty bowls.

"Why don't you two go play with the other kids? I think they're about ready to start the three-legged race over by the old outhouses."

Dory lowered her head.

"I just want to watch right now," Dory answered.

"That's okay, child. You and Mac can watch and then join in when you want."

We meandered over to an old tree stump away from the noise of the games. Dory watched Aunt Holly help clean the tables, rinse bowls and silverware.

"I guess I should help," she said.

I reached down and scratched my ankle where a chigger had decided to make its home.

"Why?" I asked. "Aunt Holly would tell you if she wanted you to help."

"I don't know. Holly is so nice."

Dory turned to look at me.

"I'm glad your dad is going to be okay."

Guilt rushed up from my gut and I gave an involuntary shudder. I really hadn't thought about my dad that much. There were quick memory flashes that soon passed. It was like nothing was wrong at times. Aunt Holly had heard from my mom on Monday and then yesterday and I'd basically put my dad and mom to one side because I had other matters to take care of that seemed more important.

"I am too."

There was silence as Dory realized she'd struck a nerve with me. I watched the sack race while Dory kept tabs on Aunt Holly. Two girls had jumped out and taken the lead the minute they heard the word Go! Leaving the boys behind, the two girls laughed as they saw the boys tumble over in their haste to catch up. One girl's blonde hair hung down in ringlets and bounced up and down as she hopped. Her whole demeanor was one of happiness. The other was shorter with bobbed black hair and worn overalls. A loud scream was heard when they crossed the finish line together.

"They're having fun," Dory said.

"Uh-huh."

"I like being with Holly," she said.

"She likes you," I said.

"She said I could live with her."

"That's good."

A slight pause ensued while Dory reached down and wiped a dirt smudge from her leg.

"I hope my little brother can come live with her too."

You could have knocked me over with a piece of straw. My mouth flew open and before I could think, I incredulously asked, "Brother?"

Dory clamped a hand over my mouth and I again got the look. I think it was then that I began to understand that the "look" didn't just mean to shut it. It also meant for me to not be so stupid. Another learning experience I would carry with me to this day.

"Shush, Mac. You may be a city boy but you got no sense!"

Crushed, I turned away and muttered, "I'm so sorry, princess." Suddenly a pain in my left arm was unbearable. "Oh! You pinched me!"

Dory giggled and her eyes sparkled like they had that first day I met her on the playground. I was completely disarmed.

"Maybe you'll listen Mr. city boy instead of shouting out."

I rubbed the back of my arm.

"You surprised me. You never said you had a brother."

Becoming pensive, she said, "I ain't seen him for four years. He was seven when the sheriff took him away."

I inched closer to her and whispered, "Why did they take him away?"

Dory's face clouded over and her eyes were cold. She clenched her fists and pounded them against her legs.

"Tony and his mother beat him. He ran away to a neighbor. They called the sheriff."

"Why didn't they take you?"

"They hid me from the sheriff. Soon after, we moved away and I don't know what happened to him."

My arm instinctively moved around and rested on her shoulders. Dory leaned against me.

"I can't think about what it would be like to lose your brother."

"I cried a lot. Every night I cried until I couldn't cry no more. I ain't got no tears left. If I find him, I want him to be with me."

Someone had brought a phonograph and placed it on a table. A stack of 45 records sat on a makeshift record holder. A bunch of the kids around my age were quickly going through the records under the frustrated supervision of one of the mothers. One of the men had plugged an extension cord from the string of lights for the phonograph.

"We can't play them all at the same time!" the woman said.

I turned to Dory.

"I hope you find him. I know John and Aunt Holly will help."

"You think they will?"

Her eyes welled with tears. Finally, Dory Grace was letting go of her feelings and becoming a regular girl.

"I know so," I said.

About that time, I saw Kelly Duncan's truck barreling down the road like he was being chased by the devil. I stood up and watched the truck pull into the schoolyard. I crammed my hands in my pocket as Kelly jumped out and searched the crowd. He saw Aunt Holly and started toward her. I glanced at Dory but she didn't seem to notice. Her eyes were on two little girls in front of her playing jump rope. Kelly gestured and Aunt Holly whipped around and scanned the crowd. I waved and she ran toward us.

"What's wrong Aunt Holly?" I asked.

She clutched my arms. Her eyes were filled with fear. I'd never seen Aunt Holly like this before.

"You and Dory have to leave with us right now. Don't worry about the dishes or the box. Just get up and go to Kelly's truck and get in the back."

Dory sat like a stone, her eyes widening in alarm. She shook her head back and forth. Tears flowed down her cheeks as she stared at Aunt Holly in disbelief.

"Tony," she whispered.

I read all the faces and shook my head in denial.

"No! He's in the jail!"

Aunt Holly gulped and placed her hands on my cheeks.

"He escaped. Early this morning."

"How could he escape?" I yelled.

Aunt Holly put a hand on my chest. "Settle down. Everything is going to be all right."

Kelly Duncan stepped forward with his hands in the back pockets of his jeans.

"The sheriff and I were called to Hickory County to track down those same cattle rustlers from the other day. We were working with the State Troopers and the Hickory County Sheriff. Early this morning after I left, the sheriff's wife took Tony his food and somehow he got the keys from her. I don't know the particulars. He tied her up and we didn't find her until thirty minutes ago when we got back to town."

The foot slipping behind the tool shed this morning had been Tony. Now I was sure of it. Why hadn't he shown himself this morning when he knew the sheriff and Kelly were gone?

"We need to get in Kelly's truck and go back to the house," Aunt Holly said.

"No!" Dory screamed. Aunt Holly pushed by me and wrapped an arm around her shoulders. Dory pulled away. "He's going to kill us all."

The two little girls stopped jumping rope and stared at Dory. Aunt Holly grabbed her arm and pulled her close again.

"Nothing is going to happen. Kelly is going to stay at our place tonight.Tomorrow morning, someone will come by and take his place. They know he's going to stay near you so they'll post a guard with us. Tomorrow the state troopers and some others are going to search for him. Everything is going to be okay."

Kelly stepped up and touched Aunt Holly's shoulder.

"We need to go now."

Aunt Holly shook her head. She gently led the weeping Dory toward Kelly's truck.

30

The moon was on the down side of full but still lit up the yard with an eerie brilliance. Kelly parked his truck in the driveway in front of the house. Aunt Holly had fixed a pot of coffee and taken a thermos to Kelly on the porch to help him stay awake. He'd been up all day walking farm fields and wooded hills searching for clues. Now he sat comfortably in the rocking chair with the porch light on and a shotgun across his legs. Miss Murphy had refused to go home. She sat in the kitchen comforting Dory. Aunt Holly busied herself by double-checking the house to make sure all the windows were closed and locked. Scooter kept nuzzling me and whining.

"What's wrong, Scooter?"

Deep inside I believed he smelled or heard Tony. They say that dogs have real good hearing and can smell anything. Aunt Holly came into the living room and stood behind me.

"You going to feed that dog?" she asked.

"Oh, my God! I forgot to feed Scooter before we went to the ice cream social."

I scrambled into the kitchen and got dog food out of the icebox. Standing at the counter, I opened the box while he jumped up and down on my leg. Nudging Scooter away, I scooped food into his bowl. He had it eaten almost before I could get it out of the box.

"Don't take him outside to go potty," Aunt Holly said. "I'm putting some papers down in here so if he starts, just pick him up and bring him in the kitchen."

I nodded my head, relieved that I wouldn't have to take Scooter outside. I sat back down at the front window and stared out into the night. My eyes searched the shadows for movement. I could tell that Kelly was uneasy on the front porch. He lit one cigarette after another and one hand nervously clutched the stock of the shotgun. Miss Murphy was asleep on the sofa while Dory lay curled in the chair with a blanket over her head.

"Why don't you try to sleep?" Aunt Holly rubbed a hand through my hair. "You look tired."

"I'd just lie there," I said. "Is Dory okay?"

Aunt Holly knelt down beside me and rested her chin on the window frame.

"I don't know if that child will ever be all right." She cocked her head to one side to peek at Kelly and then turned to lean her back against the wall. "She's changed a lot in the last week, you know."

I nodded. "Yeah, I know. She told me tonight she has a little brother."

Aunt Holly leaned forward and laid an arm on one knee.

"She did? I didn't know that."

"I didn't either. She told me tonight at the ice cream social. She wants her brother to come live with you and John."

Aunt Holly didn't answer right away. She moved and rested her chin on her knees and stared out the window.

"I don't know what to say. I'd have to talk to John..."

Aunt Holly stood up and went to the kitchen, leaving me to stare into the darkness. The filtered moonlight breaking through the trees was mesmerizing. Kelly's head bounced up now and again as the steady rhythm of the rocking chair lulled him to sleep. I'd bang on the window and he'd awake with a start, give me a sheepish grin, and take another slug of coffee from the thermos.

The clock in the kitchen chimed one o'clock. Aunt Holly came back to the window and looked out at Kelly.

"Is he doing okay? Do I need to make some more coffee?"

"Wouldn't hurt," I said. "He's tired. I've banged the window a couple of times to wake him up."

Aunt Holly rubbed her hands on her thighs and exhaled. "It's late. You need to go to bed."

"I'm not sleepy."

"Okay. A little bit longer. I'm going into the kitchen and make Kelly some more coffee."

One minute the moon flooded the whole front yard with a white light, the next it was dark as though someone had switched off a light. Kelly stood up, cradling the shotgun in his arms. Walking to the edge of the porch, he raised his face to the darkened sky before turning back around and seeing me.

"Clouds moving in," he said, pointing toward the sky. "Bet it still don't rain."

Kelly took a step toward the chair when a dark object sailed out of nowhere and struck him on the back of the head. I could hear the impact on bone and saw him fall to his knees. The shotgun tumbled from his arms and landed on the porch with a loud bang. Kelly stared at me with a helpless look. Neither he nor I could fathom what had happened. Kelly groaned. I watched him struggle to stand and then fall face down on the porch. Behind him, a figure emerged from the shadows running toward the porch.

Tony!

I mouthed the word because I was too petrified to say it. He ran like a jaguar: silent and fast. Before I knew it, Tony leaped onto the porch and grabbed Kelly's shotgun. With one swift motion, he maneuvered the stock to send it crashing through the front room window. I ducked my head below the window frame. I knew any minute that my life was over but there was nothing I could do. Frozen in space and time, I curled into a ball and waited for the fatal blast from the shotgun.

The wooden stock hit the window a couple of more times, showering me with glass. Somewhere behind me I heard Dory scream. Tony let out an animal howl and punched out the last of the glass in the window. The gunstock now came crashing down on my back. If he'd been able to solidly hit me, I'm positive he would have broken my back. The impact felt like someone held live electrical wires to me. There was nothing I could do but scream like a pathetic little kid. I remember thinking that I was going to die.

"I'm coming to get you, Dory," he shouted like a madman.

"He's coming in! He's coming in!" Dory screamed.

I heard footsteps running toward the window and Tony gave a surprised grunt. Something wet and warm splattered on my face and my whole body began to shake uncontrollably.

Aunt Holly's defiant voice filled the room.

"Take that you son-of-a-bitch!"

The shotgun fell from Tony's hands and clattered through the window, landing on the floor by my head. I didn't dare look up. There was a scuffling of feet, another grunt, and the sound of Tony falling back onto the porch floor. The rest is a blur in my memory: running feet, Dory crying hysterically, and Aunt Holly crouching beside me.

"Miss Murphy, get Dory calmed down while I look at Mac." Warm, gentle hands lifted my shirt and glided across my trembling body. "It's going to be okay, Mac. You are going to have a bruise and some minor cuts. Just consider yourself lucky. Now sit up. I need to talk to you." Her hands pulled at my shirt collar until I was in a sitting position, my back against the wall.

"Is he... is he gone?" I asked, gulping for air.

"For now."

"It was Tony this morning, wasn't it?"

"I suppose so," Aunt Holly whispered.

"Why did he wait?"

"He wanted the night. The night gives him an advantage."

Aunt Holly picked up the shotgun in one hand. On the floor rested a small, mini pitchfork on a long wooden pole. The tips were covered in blood, as was the floor around me. Aunt Holly saw my eyes focus on the object.

"I use that to gig for frogs. John left it on the back porch. For once, I'm gonna thank him for not putting something away."

"Is he dead?" I asked, looking at the swath of blood coating the floor by the window.

"No. I think I hurt him pretty bad, though. We can't take any chances. That boy isn't like normal people. Something is different about him. Some craziness keeps him going. I don't know but I expect him to return. We'll be waiting for him," she said grimly and patted the shotgun.

"Dory keeps him going," I said.

"I suspect you're right," Aunt Holly said, glancing over her shoulder at Miss Murphy and Dory.

Dory sat on the couch directly across from me. Her head was buried in Miss Murphy's shoulder and the sobs were silent.

"What about Kelly?" I asked. "We can't leave him out there."

"We're going to bring him in now." Aunt Holly helped me to my feet. "Thank goodness you're all right."

"Because of you," I said.

"Miss Murphy! I need you to help Mac pull Kelly inside."

I was filled with apprehension as Miss Murphy and I stood before the closed door. Behind us Aunt Holly readied the shotgun.

"Turn out the light," Aunt Holly whispered. She didn't want Tony to see what we were doing.

I reached for the switch and the room went dark. With the cloud cover, the front yard was an impenetrable pool of black.

"What if he comes back?" I asked.

I could hear Aunt Holly slap the shotgun with her hand.

"I'll be ready," she said. "Now open the door and let's get Kelly."

I inched the front door open and Miss Murphy and I slid out into the darkness, Aunt Holly rigid in the doorway like a prison guard. Miss Murphy and I tugged at Kelly's limp body. Dory had followed us and squatted down behind Aunt Holly. She wrapped her arms around Aunt Holly's leg like a small child. She had been on that emotional roller coaster for so long it just seemed to get worse now that Tony had returned.

"He's heavy," I said, struggling with his legs.

Miss Murphy crouched down, her hands gently supporting his head.

"If you can pull, I'll keep his head from dragging," she said.

I tugged on his legs and he didn't move.

"Dory," I said between grunts, "can you help us?"

Aunt Holly nodded and whispered something to her. Dory crept forward and took his other leg. Any minute I expected a rock to come flying through the air and hit one of us. We pulled and tugged and finally Kelly's body began to inch toward the front door. It took a great deal of effort but we finally got him through the front door. I started to close it when I saw his cap had fallen on the porch. I started to retrieve it.

"No," Aunt Holly hissed. "Leave his cap."

Thankfully, we closed the door.

"He's got a big knot on the back of his head," Miss Murphy said.

With the shotgun still in her arms, Aunt Holly pointed at a cedar chest sitting against the far wall.

"Mac, push that cedar chest over in front of the window. We'll pile something on top of it so if Tony wants to come in through the window he'll have to make a lot of noise." She shot a glance at Dory. "I want you to get on the telephone and tell the operator that Kelly is hurt. We need the sheriff out here pronto."

I thought Dory would protest. She nodded and walked cautiously into the kitchen and picked up the phone. I pushed the chest across the floor and lined it up in front of the window. Miss Murphy had gone into the bathroom and retrieved a wet towel to brush Kelly's face. I heard Dory in the kitchen turning the small crank on the side of the telephone to get the operator.

"What can we put on top of the cedar chest?" I asked.

Aunt Holly searched the room and glanced behind her toward the kitchen.

"Get that old rocking chair and John's tall ash tray and pile them on the cedar chest. In fact, pile anything you can on there and make it as high as you can. It won't keep him out but it will slow him and at least we'll hear him. We're going to barricade ourselves in the kitchen."

I got the rocking chair and the ashtray and lined them up on the cedar chest followed by a small end table and a lamp. It didn't look real secure but like Aunt Holly said, we'd hear him if he tried to come in the window. I went to the kitchen for another chair. Dory's back was to me with the telephone pressed against her ear.

"Hello? Hello? Can you hear me?"

"What's wrong?"

Dory turned to me, her face drained of all color and stared blankly at the receiver.

"It's dead," she said.

"What do you mean it's dead?" I asked.

"It's the beginning of the end," she said, handing the phone to me.

I held the receiver to my ear: nothing. Dory's hand reached out, plucked the receiver from me, and gently placed it back on its cradle. I expected her to start screaming and crying but her whole demeanor was one of acceptance. I would rather have her terrified and carrying on than this total, defeated acceptance. Dory knew Tony better than anyone and she was telling me there was no hope. Tony would kill us all. I rushed back to the living room. Miss Murphy had placed a blanket over Kelly and looked up as I ran in the room.

"They coming?" she asked.

"The phone's dead," I replied in a hushed voice.

The two women were silent for a second and then carried on as they had been. At first I thought they hadn't heard me. Aunt Holly was walking around Kelly, the shotgun hanging loosely in her arm. Miss Murphy had carefully rolled the deputy over and placed a blanket under him. Kelly didn't stir.

"Make sure that blanket is under his head good, and put that small pillow from the sofa under his head too. We've got to move him into the kitchen," Aunt Holly instructed. She handed the shotgun to me and grabbed Kelly by his heels. "Keep that shotgun ready, Mac. You've shot a twenty-two before. This one just has a little more kick."

The pillow in place, Aunt Holly grunted as she tugged on the blanket. Miss Murphy got up to help her.

"Mac, go make sure the kitchen door is locked!" Miss Murphy cried.

"And lodge a chair under the handle," Aunt Holly added.

"He can still break in the window," I said.

"But we've got the shotgun," Aunt Holly grunted.

"You already shot at Tony. We don't have any more shells," I said.

Aunt Holly didn't look at me, she just barked, "Just do what I tell you and enough with the talk!"

I ran to the backdoor expecting to see Tony staring in with that chilling grin on his face. The door was already locked, so I planted the kitchen chair securely under the doorknob. I picked up the shotgun and looked at Dory. It was disquieting to see her sit at the kitchen table with her hands calmly folded in her lap.

"Do you have any shells for that shotgun?" she asked.

I shrugged and broke the shotgun open. A new shell had been placed in the barrel. Aunt Holly did have shells.

"Got one," I said.

"Are you my friend?" she asked.

"Well--yeah."

"Do you think you could shoot me with that shotgun?"

Her voice was calm, almost singsong when she spoke. I glared at her incredulously.

"What are you talking about? That's plain dumb!" I shouted.

"No one's shooting anyone," Aunt Holly panted, pulling Kelly through the doorway. "Miss Murphy, soon as we get him through the door close it and brace a chair against the doorknob."

"It's dark in here," I said. "Do you want to turn on the lights?"

Aunt Holly sat down in a chair, her chest heaving, and her breath chugging like a locomotive. She wiped her forehead with her arm while looking around the kitchen.

"Look in the pantry and see if you can find an oil lamp. It should be in the back sitting on the top shelf. If you can't reach it, I'll get it. We use it when we have bad storms and the electricity goes out."

"Why do you want that for?" asked Miss Murphy.

"'Cause he's going to knock the lights out," she replied in a matter of fact tone of voice. "He's got the phone out so the next step is to take down the lights."

"You think he can do that?" Miss Murphy asked.

I was already in the pantry, a four by eight room where Aunt Holly kept all her canned goods and extra eggs. It smelled musty and sour from what remained of the old potatoes she and John used in the spring to seed their garden. A single bulb hung in the middle of the room with a long string hanging down. I pulled the string and felt a surge of relief as a dim light came on. I didn't want Tony to turn off the lights. I found the oil lamp and a box of wooden matches and returned to the kitchen to find Aunt Holly holding the shotgun. Three shotgun shells sat on end beside a box on the kitchen table.

"We have four shells left," she said. "It only takes one to kill him."

"You hurt him when he was coming in the window," I said.

"Yes, I got him and there was blood all over everywhere. He should be hurting."

"You don't know Tony," Dory interrupted. "He's not like anybody I've ever seen. He don't feel pain like we do."

"You mean he couldn't feel that buckshot?" I asked.

"He could feel it but not the same. Especially when he's real angry.

When he gets angry he feels nothing but getting even."

"Maybe we could go to my house and call," Miss Murphy said.

"Thanks, but no thanks." Aunt Holly answered, kneeling down and pressing her fingers around Kelly's wrist to check his blood pressure. Her eyes met Miss Murphy, who sat stroking Kelly's hair. "The night belongs to Tony and I don't want him to hurt anyone else. Let's wait until morning. Then the sheriff should be out here to relieve Kelly."

A loud crackling noise came from outside and the lights went out. Aunt Holly's hopeful words were swallowed by darkness.

31

We sat in the darkened kitchen and waited. Only the sounds of our breathing, the obnoxious croaking frogs, and the occasional chair scraping on the floor broke the silence. Aunt Holly positioned her chair in front of the sink and in-between the doors to the back porch and the living room. I sat near her, one hand clutching a box of matches and the other the oil lamp. Dory remained silent beside me. Moonlight leaked through the tall elm trees outside the kitchen window, providing our only light. I could barely make out Dory's form as her right hand nervously wrapped and unwrapped a swath of hair behind her ear. Miss Murphy sat near the icebox, her face lost in the shadows. We said nothing. Finally Aunt Holly got out of her chair and stood to one side of the kitchen window and peered out into the shifting shadows of the yard.

"What is it, Holly?" Miss Murphy whispered.

Before Aunt Holly could answer, a heavy rock shot through the kitchen window, shattering it into a million pieces. The rock bounced off the kitchen table and barely missed Dory and me.

"No!" screamed Dory.

"Get down under the table!" Aunt Holly ordered.

"He's got that slingshot," I shouted.

I tugged on Dory's arm and yanked her out of the chair. She tumbled under the table just as another rock came hurtling through the window and crashed into her chair. Miss Murphy stood up and moved in the shadows toward Aunt Holly. Her arm rose and pointed toward the window.

"I see him," she whispered. He's not twenty-five feet away from the house."

Aunt Holly ducked down and joined Miss Murphy on the other side of the kitchen window.

"Where?"

Miss Murphy pulled Aunt Holly in front of her and then laid her arm over Aunt Holly's shoulder and pointed.

"There."

"I see him."

"You going shoot him?" I asked in a hushed voice.

"He's too far," she answered. "With the trees and everything, it isn't going to do any damage."

Miss Murphy peered around Aunt Holly's shoulder.

"What's that on his right arm?"

"Watch out. Here comes another rock," Aunt Holly said.

This time it hit the window frame and ricocheted back into the yard.

"He's got his left arm in a sling," Miss Murphy said. "He's got his leg wrapped, too. You must have gigged him pretty good."

Aunt Holly positioned herself so she could look closer.

"Looks like he has a tourniquet on it," she said.

Miss Murphy drew closer to the window.

"He can't use his left arm very well. So you did hurt him. That's going to make it harder for him to get inside."

"His arm is well enough to shoot rocks at us with that slingshot," Aunt Holly replied.

Dory's muted voice came from under the table.

"You don't understand Tony. It don't matter what happens to him. When he wants something, he'll do anything to get it."

I held my breath as Aunt Holly stepped in front of the window in plain view, the shotgun raised to her shoulder. The blast was deafening, echoing throughout the small kitchen even as a third missile hit the table, barely missing Aunt Holly. A cry of agony and a bloodthirsty scream came from outside.

"You got him!" Miss Murphy cried.

"Not good enough," Aunt Holly replied. "It will give us a little time while he picks buckshot out of his chest."

"Everyone okay?" Miss Murphy asked.

I crawled out from underneath the kitchen table. Dory scooted across the floor and clung to Aunt Holly's leg.

"You are so brave," she said.

Aunt Holly pulled her up and threw her arms around her.

"Not as brave as you. You've lived with that monster. Now, both of you get back under that table and stay there."

The night dragged on. Miss Murphy and Aunt Holly took turns watching out the window while Dory and I huddled under the table.

"Do you think he'll try and break in again, Aunt Holly?" I asked.

"I don't know, Mac. I just don't know."

"He will," Dory said.

"Well, we have three more shotgun shells, so he'd better not try," said Miss Murphy.

"We know his arm and leg are hurt where I got him with the gigging fork. He has his arm in a makeshift sling. Just now I got him with some buckshot in the chest but it's more of a bother. It really didn't do any damage."

"So what's he waiting for?" asked Miss Murphy.

"He doesn't know how many shotgun shells we have, so he's going to wait as long as he can. We have no phone. Our only hope is Kelly's replacement, whoever that is," answered Aunt Holly. "Right now, time is on his side."

"What time is it?" I asked.

"Four o'clock," Aunt Holly answered. "Not much longer to sun up."

"What happens when it gets light?" I asked.

Miss Murphy scooted her chair closer to me. "We're going to march over to my house and call the sheriff."

"What about the truck?" I asked.

"He's flattened the tires," Aunt Holly answered.

"Maybe I should tell Tony I'll go with him. He won't kill nobody then," Dory said.

"No!" barked Aunt Holly and Miss Murphy in unison.

Miss Murphy dropped to the floor and peered at Dory under the table. "You'll do no such thing, child. Don't even think about it."

Around five o'clock Kelly moaned. It had gotten a little darker outside as the moon started its slide down in the sky and began to sink behind the treetops. I think we'd forgotten about Kelly. Miss Murphy had folded a wet towel on his forehead and placed a few tablecloths over him. Aunt Holly had placed a kitchen chair upside down over his head to he wouldn't be hit by one of Tony's rocks. When he moaned, I about jumped out of my skin. It was eerie to have the charged silence broken by the mournful sound.

"Move the chair, Mac, while Miss Murphy takes a look at him."

Miss Murphy knelt by his side and stroked Kelly's hair.

"Kelly, can you hear me?"

Kelly rolled his head and moaned again.

"Mac, light that oil lamp so we can see," Aunt Holly said.

I took off the chimney and struck a match. It wouldn't light.

"Mac, turn that knob on the side of the lamp. That will make the wick stick out a little further so you can light it," Miss Murphy said.

I nodded to Miss Murphy, although I doubted she could see me that well, and turned the knob. The match burned my fingers so I dropped it on the floor.

"Ow!"

"Try it again," said Aunt Holly.

I struck another match and the head busted off and disappeared in the darkness. I pulled out another match and this time it flared when scratched across the side of the matchbox. The wick lit and gave off a warm yellow glow.

"Bring it closer, Mac," said Miss Murphy.

I knelt down beside her as she placed her hands on Kelly's cheeks.

"Kelly, can you hear me?"

She rolled his head to one side and patted his cheeks. The eyelids fluttered to reveal eyes rolled up in the back of his head. Even in the yellow glow of the oil lamp, Kelly had a pale, gray skin color. He took short, gasping breaths. Above his left temple he had a knot almost the size of a baseball.

"Dory. Come get this glass of water and see if we can get him to take a little drink," Aunt Holly said.

Dory handed the glass to Miss Murphy.

"Just put it on his lips," Aunt Holly said.

"Kelly, I'm going to rub a teensy bit of water on your lips."

She dipped her forefinger in the glass and then rubbed his lips with her wet finger. Kelly's eyelids fluttered again and this time his eyes dropped down and stared vacantly straight ahead. Miss Murphy dipped her finger again and rubbed across his lips. His tongue pushed out between his lips and he began to lick.

"That a boy," Miss Murphy said.

She continued rubbing his lips until finally Kelly started to look around.

"Ow," he groaned.

"Take it easy, Kelly. You took a hard hit to the temple. You might have a concussion. Let's see if you can take a small sip of water."

Miss Murphy clasped her hand on the back of Kelly's head and pulled him up. The glass touched his lips and he hungrily mouthed the rim.

"Not so fast, Kelly. Not so fast. Little at a time. Little at a time. That's right."

Aunt Holly turned on the water and was surprised to find that the electricity was still on in the pump house. She wet a tee towel, handed it to Dory, and nodded toward Kelly. Dory knelt down beside him and began to wipe his face with the damp cloth. Kelly's hands grabbed Dory's and his whole body began to shake.

"Where... where am I," he asked in a desperate voice.

"You're at Holly's place, remember?" Miss Murphy answered, gently rubbing his head. "You're going to be all right."

Kelly shook his head and closed his eyes. Miss Murphy gently placed his head back on the small pillow and looked over at Aunt Holly.

"I think he's going out again. He needs a doctor real bad."

Aunt Holly turned to look out the window. A halo of light began to peek over the horizon.

"I know," she said. "It will be light enough in another half-hour that we can go to your house and call."

"What about Kelly? I asked. "He can't go in this condition."

"We'll have to leave him," she said quietly.

"Tony will kill him," I objected.

"I don't think so," she answered. "He wants Dory. He wants us. Kelly hasn't done anything to make Tony mad."

Dory shivered and curled her legs up under her chin.

32

We gathered at the kitchen door. Aunt Holly explained how we would go in a group, not single file. That way it would be harder for Tony to pick one person to hit with his slingshot. She'd picked up a shotgun shell from the table and loaded it into the barrel. The other shell she tucked into her blouse pocket. The watch Aunt Holly gave me earlier in the week pointed to six o'clock. Miss Murphy had taken a carving knife out of a kitchen drawer and slipped it in her large bag. I glanced down at Kelly Duncan on the floor. A kitchen chair no longer covered his face. Miss Murphy removed the pillow from under his head and replaced it with a rolled up towel that fit into the crook of his neck so his head wouldn't move. His feet were slightly elevated on a round, aluminum dishpan. Miss Murphy had covered him with an old cotton quilt.

"Is he going to be all right?" Dory asked.

Miss Murphy looked sadly at Kelly. "I'm afraid he's in shock. We need to get him medical attention as fast as possible."

"It looks like his head is swelling," I said.

"Come on, now," Aunt Holly shushed us. "We have to talk about how were are going to get to Miss Murphy's house. If we don't try, Kelly isn't going to get the help he needs."

"What if we just wait for the sheriff?" Dory asked.

"The sun is up. Tony knows that time is running out. He's going to make his move very shortly. This way we're not all corraled together. If he gets one of us, the others can still make it to Miss Murphy's house. She left the back door unlocked, so we'll go around back when we get there."

"What will we do if once outside, Tony attacks us?" asked Miss Murphy.

"Run. Run for your lives."

I raised my hand in disbelief.

"You mean if he hits you, you want me to just leave you there?"

"Yes. Unless you think you have time to pick up the shotgun and shoot the son-of-a-bitch. Now, let's go over the plan."

"Do I have to leave Scooter?" I asked.

"I don't like the idea of leaving Scooter and Kelly," Dory moaned.

"I don't think we have much choice," Aunt Holly said. "Now, let's get on with it. Mac will pull the chair away from the kitchen door and swing it open wide. We'll wait a couple of seconds to see if Tony comes rushing in. If he does, me and this old shotgun will be waiting for him. Mac, you must remember to jump back once you open the door. Okay?"

I reluctantly nodded my head. I didn't like the idea of leaving the kitchen.

"If Tony doesn't come barging in, I'll lead the way out into the living room and the rest will follow. Miss Murphy will be last and you kids will be between us. We'll do the same at the front door. Once we are all outside, we'll walk in a diamond. Dory will lead and Mac will bring up the rear. Miss Murphy and I will walk on the sides."

I think we were all in a daze that morning. I moved the chair barring the door into the living room and threw the door open. It banged against the wall with a loud thud as I jumped back. Aunt Holly waited for a few seconds. With the shotgun leveled straight ahead, shifted her weight and peered around the corner to make sure Tony was not waiting for us before she stepped into the living room. Seeing that it was clear, she motioned for us to follow. Everything looked as it had the night before. A chair was hooked under the front doorknob, the chest and tables were stacked in front of the window, and splattered blood was was drying on the floor. I wondered how Aunt Holly would get the stain out of the wood. The floor creaked under our steps and shattered the silence of the morning. Aunt Holly stood to one side of the front door and motioned to me. I pulled the chair out and threw open the front door, forgetting to jump back. We waited to see if anything would happen. Aunt Holly leveled the shotgun at the front door and nodded to me again. I ran to the front window, as Aunt Holly had told me to do earlier, and carefully took the chair down and quietly placed it on the floor. I stretched to look both ways out the window onto the porch and saw nothing. I nodded and she proceeded outside. We stood on the porch and waited: nothing happened.

"Too quiet," whispered Miss Murphy. "I don't hear the birds."

"Maybe that's why," I said, pointing toward a dead blue jay beside the steps.

"Tony likes killing birds with his slingshot," Dory said in a flat tone.

"Okay, let's go," Aunt Holly said, stepping off the porch.

We formed a tight little band as Aunt Holly had instructed, moving slowly, constantly searching for any sign of Tony. Fifteen feet from the porch Miss Murphy screamed in pain and fell to the ground.

"Ow, my leg!" she cried, unable to hold back the tears.

I saw Tony at the edge of the house, his shirt off, his arm and one leg covered by makeshift bandages. His slingshot hung from one hand. The shotgun blasted beside my head but Tony had already disappeared around the side of the house.

"Damn!" Aunt Holly muttered, breaking the shotgun, tossing out the old shell and replacing a new one. She then crouched down by Miss Murphy. "How are you?"

"Run! You have to get away," Miss Murphy moaned. "You don't have much time."

I had become frantic because I remembered what Tony did to me in the schoolyard and how he'd butchered that little calf. My whole body trembled as my eyes darted back and forth, searching for him. Dory brushed up against me and threaded her arm through mine. I could feel her pulse beat as her fingers clawed into my flesh.

"Can you stand up?" Aunt Holly asked.

"Take your own advice and run," Miss Murphy moaned.

"I still have one or two shells left," Aunt Holly said.

"If he comes back, run to the pond and get in the boat," Dory whispered in my ear.

"Why?" I asked.

"Tony can't swim. He's afraid of the water. And we'll never make it to Miss Murphy's. We wasted too much time."

I wondered if we could outrun Tony all the way to the pond.

"He still has the slingshot," I insisted.

"I know. We can keep rowing away from him. It's our only hope."

"I think I can," Miss Murphy moaned. When she attempted to stand she fell back down. "I don't know. He hit my leg hard."

Aunt Holly laid the shotgun down and held out both hands for Miss Murphy to grasp. Tony didn't let out his horrible war cry but crept silently to edge of the house. As Aunt Holly bent toward Miss Murphy he stepped out and let the rock fly. Aunt Holly had no chance to dodge. It ricocheted off the side of her head and she crumpled like a deflated balloon. She didn't even cry out.

"Wahoo!" Tony screamed.

"Run!" Dory cried as she clasped my hand and pulled me away.

"I can't leave Aunt Holly," I protested, attempting to stop her.

"He don't want Holly. He wants me and you. Run!"

We beat a path toward the pond as Tony sauntered over to where Aunt Holly and Miss Murphy lay crumpled on the ground. I turned and watched him pick up the shotgun. He stepped over Aunt Holly and started running after us.

"Don't look at him. Run!" Dory commanded.

"I coming for you, Dory. You can't get away." Tony cried out, and that was followed by a wild cackle that sent chills down my spine.

"Don't you listen to him, Mac. We got to get in that boat."

"But he has a shotgun," I said.

"Don't make no difference. He's got one shot left and if we get far out into the pond, we can't be hurt."

"I hope so," I said. My lungs felt like they were going to explode from running so fast. The old Dory had come back. This was the Dory who took charge when it came to Tony.

"I can't let him hurt you," she shouted.

We ran down the hill toward the pond faster than we'd ever run. Dory clutched my hand as we rounded the far side of the pond to the small dock and the johnboat. I stopped and caught my breath, turning to look for Tony. With his leg all banged up, I thought he'd be slowed but he was already halfway around the large pond. Dory had run out on the dock and untied the boat. She crawled into the johnboat and grabbed a paddle. "Come on, Mac. He's almost here," she said, urgency and fear mingling in her voice.

Tony had closed the gap and would be on us by the time I got in the boat. Taking three large steps to the end of the dock, I grabbed the edge of the johnboat and sent it backward into the pond. I fell down on my stomach in the process and lay spread-eagled on the dock.

"No!" Dory screamed.

"Paddle, Dory. Paddle hard!" I shouted.

The butt of the shotgun found its mark between my shoulder blades. The pain was so intense that I almost blacked out. A loud grunt gushed from my mouth as my head slammed against the dock. Through half-closed eyes I saw the johnboat drift slowly toward the middle of the pond. Dory had her hands over her eyes. I kept my eyes on Dory, thinking this was the last time I'd ever see her.

That is when I heard Tony's menacing voice above me.

"Hey, Dory. I gonna shoot boyfriend here. You wanna watch?"

One hand grabbed my arm and flipped me over. He straddled me and brought the shotgun to his shoulder. I could see the red marks where his chest was peppered with buckshot. "I need you to watch, Dory."

I realized now that I should be the one in that johnboat because Tony would never kill Dory. She knew that and she had been trying to save me. I searched Tony's face for any hint of mercy and saw only hatred and a raw animal anger. His only thought was to strike back at whoever had invaded his life and taken the only thing that mattered to him - Dory. His finger tightened on the trigger. His eye squinted as he took aim. A soft cackle escaped his lips. He was truly enjoying the moment. I closed my eyes and held my breath. I can't remember if I was scared. Sometimes the unknown frightens us but once it becomes known, the fear goes away. I don't know if that is what happened to me. I just knew that it would soon be over.

"I wouldn't do that, son."

My eyes burst open. Everett Jackson stood at the end of the dock, his own shotgun leveled at Tony. Everett looked like he did a couple of days ago: grizzled, shirtless, a baseball hat askew on his head. My heart pounded as a glimmer of hope started to thread its way through my body. Tony's body tensed. His tongue played across his sharpened teeth as his eyes darted from me to Dory in the boat. He adjusted his hands on the shotgun . I could tell Tony was mulling over what to do. His arms twitched and he began to bite at his lower lip. Suddenly, a smile spread across his face and I knew he'd made a decision. I couldn't close my eyes, even though he might pull the trigger and kill me.

"Tony, please don't hurt him," Dory whimpered from the boat. "I'll come back."

Tony stared long and hard at Dory in the johnboat. I could only imagine what was going through his mind. If he killed me, Everett would shoot him. Even if he turned to kill Everett, his chances of living were poor. There was a cry and a large black crow flew overhead. I heard Dory sobbing, her muttering incomprehensible. Everything centered on what Tony would decide.

"Put the gun down, boy. I've got a clear shot."

Tony quickly whirled around, dropped to one knee. The blast was deafening. My eyes were on Everett who stood with the butt of his shotgun wedged against his waist. Tony's shot had missed by a mile. Everett's response was immediate. Smoke shot from the barrel and my legs felt like they were hit with a thousand stabbing needles. The shotgun flew from Tony's hands and his scream echoed mine. He fell backward and clawed at the air to catch his balance. He landed on top of me. His face hit mine and for the first time I saw agony written all over it. The force of the blast rolled him toward the edge of the dock. Realizing what was happening, he grabbed at the only thing between him and the water. I stiffened my body as his hands found my arm and my body began to slide off the dock into the water.

The water felt warm. I opened my eyes and saw that the underside of the floating dock was a dark green. I hit bottom, landing on a scrap pile of old Christmas trees that John had placed there for fish cover. I couldn't see Tony. My legs pushed hard against the bottom and I kicked toward the surface. I'd never realized the depth at this end. It was easily fifteen feet. Suddenly, a clawing at my legs stopped my progress. I kicked as hard as I could and started again toward the surface but was stopped again by a frantic Tony. His hands clawed up my body and I saw sheer terror on his face as he passed. His chest was oozing blood. I'll never know how he got his feet on my shoulders but that sent me shooting back toward the bottom. I must have opened my mouth in protest because my mouth filled with water. I panicked. My arms flailed in the water but I continued to sink. Sheer terror shot through me, leaving a strange calm in it's wake. I looked up at the watery light above me and kicked off the bottom again, shooting straight up. I stretched my arms over my head and brought them in a sweeping motion to my side. My head broke through to the surface.

I spit out water and coughed. I gulped and pinpricks of pain shot through me as my lungs filled with air. Wiping my eyes, I saw Tony struggling to grab the edge of the dock. Everett stood over him, his face void of any emotion. He offered no assistance. Sometimes in life you just react. You don't reason why or evaluate your actions, you just respond. Treading water, I moved in behind Tony. I heard him gasping for breath. Tony managed to clutch the edge of the dock and Everett brought his boot firmly down on his fingers. I reached out and placed my hand on the top of his head. Tony was so frantic he didn't even feel my hand. He was tiring and I heard him give a slight whimper. My hand pushed down and his head turned. His eyes met mine. All the hate and anger were gone, leaving only fear. I grasped the edge of the dock and hoisted myself up so I could press down that much harder. You would have thought that Tony would put up more resistance in his final moments. His mouth opened one last time to call for help or maybe he wanted to ask for mercy. The greenish pond water rushed into his mouth and muffled whatever he'd wanted to say. He surfaced again, his head pushing hard against my hand. He gulped, made one last attempt to grab the edge of the dock and then slowly began to sink to the bottom of the pond. I felt a hand grab at my leg but I kicked it off.

Everett pulled me out of the water and I collapsed on the weathered boarding of the dock. My breathing came in short bursts and I couldn't control my body from shaking. The sobs followed, hard sobs that took my breath away. They were sobs of relief, sobs of guilt. I had done something to another human being that would haunt me for the rest of my life. I had taken life from another. Everett sat me up and placed his arm around me and patted my shoulder.

"This is our secret, son. You understand? No one needs to know what happened. I shot him and he fell in the water and drowned. You got that?"

I shook my head and continued to sob. Everett stood up and called Dory back.

It was over.

33

The ambulance pulled away from the house carrying Kelly to the hospital in Springfield. John sat on the front porch with Aunt Holly and Dory. He'd returned just in time to hear the shotgun blasts down by the pond. Sheriff Badger was right behind him and they'd found Miss Murphy trying to attend to Aunt Holly. Sheriff Badger had run toward the gunfire while John raced to Aunt Holly. I'll never forget the look on his face when I came up the hill toward the house with Everett carrying Dory in his arms. I don't think John knew what to say or do.

"John, Holly doesn't want to go into Springfield to the hospital. I think she should go into town and see the doc," Miss Murphy said.

John appeared to be in a daze. He couldn't comprehend what all had happened in his absence.

"Sure, sure. I'll take her. I'll take you, too."

"You sure you don't want to go to Springfield with her?" the sheriff asked.

"Yeah, I'm sure."

The sheriff slapped John on the shoulder.

"Okay, John. You get the women in the car and I'll follow. I need to find someone to drag the pond for Tony." The sheriff turned toward Everett and me sitting on the front porch. "And I'll be back to talk to you fellas."

Everyone was so worried about Aunt Holly, Miss Murphy and Dory that I had become a second thought. Everett had checked my leg for buckshot but found none had penetrated my jeans. Everett said I was lucky. Tony's body had shielded me from the worst of it. John had one foot in the car when he remembered me.

"You going to be all right with Everett?"

"Sure." I waved my hand and John got in the car and sped out of the driveway.

I went inside and found Scooter. Everett took a seat on the edge of the porch and waited for the sheriff. I returned to the front porch and sat on the old chair with Scooter snuggled in my lap, nipping at my fingers. Everett had pulled a bag of sunflower seeds out of his pocket. He would leisurely pop a single seed into his mouth, crunch down, and then spit the shell out. He didn't say anything and I tried to ignore him. If we talked I'd remember the look on Tony's face as I pushed him under the water. At the time, I thought it was the thing to do. I didn't even think about it. Automatically my arm reached out and snuffed out a life. I heard Dory scream and then she fell backward in the boat. That was what hurt the most, hearing Dory scream. At first, I didn't understand what made her scream. Did she really have some type of feelings for Tony? Later, walking up that hill behind Everett with Dory limp in his arms, I knew what bothered Dory was that she'd seen someone die.

"You okay, son?" he asked, staring straight ahead.

"I guess," I murmured.

My innocence had been taken from me that day. There was nothing I could do to bring it back. Deep down inside I wanted to run out and tell the world that I had drowned Tony Grace. Everett and I had drowned Tony. Everett had prevented Tony from pulling himself up on the dock. I'd pushed his head under the water.

Everett adjusted the strap on his overalls.

"Don't take it hard, son. He was a bad 'un. No good would have come to Dory if he'd lived. She'd always be looking over her shoulder. They would have sent him to prison but the minute he got out, he'd be heading for wherever Dory had landed. You know that, don't you?"

"I guess," I said.

Everett was right but that wasn't the way things were supposed to happen. In my young mind, Tony would get arrested and go to jail. Everyone else would live happily ever after. Isn't that the way it happens in books and at the movies? That was the moment in my life that I realized that happily ever after doesn't exist. Up until that moment, I'd never experienced the terrible things the world held in store for some. My folks certainly weren't rich but they provided the shelter that I needed to feel safe. I don't mean the shelter over your head. I mean that type of shelter that keeps you safe until your family can wean you into the world. My weaning had come to an abrupt halt and there was a dark void in my chest.

"If it's any help, I know how you feel. During the World War I killed men. I had dreams about it but then it became second nature. What bothered me the most was killing people became easy. That's when you need to worry, son. When I came home from the war, I said I ain't ever gonna kill another man, and I meant it. But today it had to be done for Dory's sake. Hell, for your sake, too."

"I just can't get that look he had in his eyes out of my mind."

"Pure terror wasn't it? He knew it was over. He'd finally lost."

"Do you think he would have killed Dory?"

Everett spit out another sunflower seed and wiped his grizzled mouth with the back of his hand.

"I don't know about that but he'd have killed you without blinking an eye."

"I know," I whispered. I gave Scooter a big hug.

"The sheriff is back already." Everett stood up to meet him. He turned and poured the remaining sunflower seeds into my hand. "Here, you finish 'em. Let me do the talking."

I looked at those sunflower seeds with disgust. Everett wasn't too tidy about washing his hands. The sheriff drove a 1949 black and white Chevy. The words Polk County Sheriff were painted in black on the white doors. There were no red lights on top but it did have a horn shaped siren mounted on the fender. The tires crunched on the gravel as the car rode the rough driveway like a ship in a swelling ocean. I started to get up but something landed on my hand and began to nibble at the sunflower seeds.

"Howard," I whispered trailing my forefinger down his back. "You know you can't eat those sunflower seeds. They're too big for you."

Howard's blue feathers looked filthy as he furiously pecked at the seeds in my hand. I pushed Scooter on the ground and picked up a seed, split it open with my thumb and offered it to Howard. I gently got up and walked to the front door. Once inside, Howard flew off my hand and landed on a floor lamp beside the sofa. I busily cracked the sunflower seeds and put them in an ashtray. Howard didn't wait for an invitation. I rushed into the kitchen and got a small coffee cup and filled it with water and placed it beside the seeds. If Howard was afraid of me, he didn't show it.

"Mac, come on out here," I heard the sheriff call.

"I'm coming," I said. Howard bobbed his head when my forefinger stroked him. "Miss Murphy is going to be happy to see you, Howard."

I walked out the front door to see the sheriff and Everett talking. The sheriff leaned against his car with his arms crossed over his chest. Everett was beside him and both men were laughing. Sheriff Badger was an older man with a large belly that overlapped his belt. A white Stetson hat was pushed back on his head. He gave a wave when I came down the front steps but didn't stop talking to Everett. As I approached, both men laughed again and Sheriff Badger slapped Everett on the shoulder.

"Come on over here, Mac," the sheriff said.

"Yes sir."

He placed a hand on my shoulder and pulled me closer.

"I'm sorry about what happened today. Everett has told me what I need to know. I just need to ask you one question. Is that okay?"

I shrugged and shoved my hands in my pockets.

"I guess so."

"Good, good. All I need to know is if you thought that Tony Thomas was going to kill you before Everett shot him?"

"Who?" I asked. "Tony Thomas?"

"That was Tony's real name, Mac," offered Everett.

"Oh."

"Now, Mac, did you feel that Tony Thomas was going to kill you when Everett had to shoot him?"

I looked from the sheriff to Everett who gave me a slight nod. I gulped and looked down at the ground.

"Yes sir."

The sheriff clapped me on the shoulder.

"That's it, son. Everett filled me in on everything that happened. You must have been scared to death when he rolled over and pulled you into the water."

I glanced again to Everett who gave me the okay.

"Yes, it was scary."

"Good thing he's dead. God knows what that kid could do to you."

I couldn't think of anything to say. I didn't want to tell the sheriff that I'd killed Tony. Everett had kept Tony from getting on the dock but I was the one that had pushed him under the water. The problem was, I really wanted to tell someone. This was the type of thing that nagged at you until you thought you were going to burst. My body squirmed inside like a tangled-up worm. If the sheriff was suspicious, he certainly didn't let on at the time. I thought I was going to die as they continued talking.

"I'm going back to get my dog," I said.

"Sure, son. Don't mind us. We're just chawing the fat here. Everett is going to stay with you until everyone gets back."

Scooter was out in the yard. Tail wagging as he attempted to pounce on a grasshopper while I marveled at his tenacity. He'd move, the grasshopper moved, and each time Scooter gave a low growl and bark. His tail wagged like a motor. I followed the two around the yard with amazement. The more that Scooter missed, the more determined he became to catch that grasshopper.

I heard a car door slam and the crunch of footsteps on the gravel behind me. "If he catches it, he won't know what to do with it," Everett laughed. "This is better than the circus."

"Come on, Scooter." I reached down and picked Scooter up in my arms. "I just realized that he hasn't had anything to eat since yesterday."

"No wonder he's after that grasshopper," Everett said. His hand reached out and gave me a gentle push.

Inside, Scooter growled at a bowl of dog food while Everett and I tried to pick up some of the mess in the living room. The blood had dried hard on the floor but the memories were vivid in my mind. The glass window that shattered, showering me with small slivers that miraculously did no harm. The thought of Tony's foot against me, although only for a second, still made me shiver. At that moment I'd thought my life was over.

"Go get a broom, Mac. A dustpan if you can find it. This is a regular mess in here. You all must have been going out of your mind with that guy outside."

My eyes met Everett's. His face hardened and his fists clinched while his bottom lip crawled up and covered his upper. The hatred he felt toward Tony was something that I'd never experienced before. I hadn't had time to become angry because I had been so frightened all the time, frightened for Dory and me. I didn't say anything in reply. I didn't know what to say. To tell the truth, I don't think I was thinking about anything at the time, just going through the motions. Glass crackled under my feet in the kitchen and I stopped to look out the jagged edges of the broken window. I saw Kelly in my mind's eye lying unconscious on the floor with his head swelling. Dory sitting in a chair with her arms clasped around her knees in fear. Aunt Holly standing at the window with the shotgun in her hand. Miss Murphy sitting quietly to one side of the kitchen, determination and defiance on her face. The living room and now the kitchen were too much for me. I began to shake uncontrollably and my head pounded like someone was hitting it with a hammer. I saw Dory sitting in the boat, her hands covering her face as Tony taunted her. Tony straddling my body and looking down at me with those dark, piercing eyes, almost salivating at the thought of killing me. Suddenly, I bent over the sink and began to dry heave. My stomach wretched until it hurt but nothing lay in the sink in front of me. It seemed like I stood there forever. Finally the wretching stopped. I straightened, gasping for air when I felt a soft hand on my shoulder. Aunt Holly stood beside me with tears in her eyes. Her arms encircled me and I fell into her embrace and began to sob.

"Let it out, Mac. Let it all out. Don't hold anything back."

My face nuzzled into her softness and out of the corner of my eye I spied John standing quietly in the doorway. Dory stood beside him. John gently pushed her and, with red-rimmed eyes, she walked slowly toward us as Aunt Holly stretched out her arm to welcome her.

34

I feel better now. All my life I've avoided thinking about that day. The awful memory from my youth has finally leeched out of my subconscious. The house is silent except for my footsteps echoing off the walls. Another door in my life has closed and a new door is opening as I start a new chapter living with my son's family. Aunt Holly and Uncle John died about twenty years ago. My parents quickly followed. My brother passed and Dory was all I had left of family.

After Tony died that summer, I continued to live with Aunt Holly and John until school started in the fall. Dory started back to school that year as well. I returned to Kansas City and she stayed in Bolivar with Aunt Holly and Uncle John. Dory's journal was given to the sheriff. Once the court read the journal, Mrs. Grace disappeared from Polk county. Aunt Holly and John made several attempts to find Dory's brother. John met with a state worker in Springfield who told him that her brother died from the measles. Dory was heart-broken over the news. I gave her Scooter when I left for home that summer. She loved that dog. They were inseparable. I was in my twenties and married when Scooter died. My wife and I came back to Bolivar for a proper burial behind the tool shed.

Dory never married. She was content to live a peaceful life on the farm. John built her a chicken coop and she raised chickens. She sold their eggs. Later, she lived on a trust fund that Uncle John and Aunt Holly had set up for her. Dory lived in peace. She read books but had no television, radio, or newspaper. The President of the United States could have been her neighbor and she wouldn't have cared less.

During my youth I visited during the summers, weekends and holidays. We were fast friends. Fishing, swimming in the pond, or playing with Scooter kept us occupied. Sometimes we would sit under the willow tree by the pond and I'd tell Dory how I wanted to become a lawyer. She listened to my dreams and encouraged me. I went to college in Springfield and came down to Bolivar often on weekends. I would tell Dory she needed to go to school with me. She always declined. I think to be content was what Dory wanted out of life. She'd faced so many challenges early on and now she was happy. After law school in Columbia, Missouri, I headed back to Kansas City and practiced law until my retirement a couple of years ago. During those working years, I married, raised a son and daughter, and returned to Bolivar as often as I could.

My wife died last year and Dory left Bolivar for the first time since that eventful summer to attend her funeral. Now I've have come to bury Dory. She never went to a doctor. She'd told me something was wrong. I begged her to go to the doctor but she was afraid they'd put her in the hospital. She died on the front porch in the rocking chair she loved so much. Even today, when I first approached the house, I saw Scooter running out the front door to meet me with his tongue hanging cockeyed out of his mouth, Dory on his heels.

"Dad? You ready?"

My son, Joel, stands at the front door with a walnut box tucked in his left arm. My daughter, Judy, stands behind him. Both look at me anxiously. My heart pounds as I shake my head and move toward the front door. Everywhere I look brings back memories and I feel a heaviness settling on my shoulders. Tears flood my eyes and Joel reaches for me. Their arms entwined in mine, my children and I walk across the red rock of Polk County toward the pond.

The willow tree looks ancient and the roots have broken the earth and lie gnarled under our feet. It still stands majestic beside the water. This is where Dory and I used to come to fish and play. This is where she told me she wanted her ashes released to the wind. I motion to Joel and he lifts the lid off the walnut box. I dip my hand in the grayish ashes. Some fall to the ground and I laugh.

"She can't wait to get back to the farm."

Joel and Judy look at each other like I'm a little crazy at the moment. Maybe I am. They haven't had to say many goodbyes. My sister of a different mother was being put to rest where she belonged. I lift my hand over my head and a slight breeze begins to blow, nipping at the ashes and taking them out of my hand. I dip my hand in again and lift it to the wind that grows a little stronger as if it was waiting for me. Dory swirls in the wind, across the pond and fields. I finally take the box from Joel and holding tight, toss what remains of her ashes in the air. I start to cry.

"Goodbye, Dory Grace. Goodbye old friend."

***

If you enjoyed this book, you might enjoy David Hooper's Tanglewood Road. You can visit the author's web site for more information.

http://www.davidmhooper.com

Made in the USA
Charleston, SC
08 June 2012